Dreaming Australia

Steve Tolbert's other young adult books are

Channeary
Settling South
Stepping Back
Eyeing Everest
Escape to Kalimantan
Tracking the Dalai Lama
Packing Smack, Talking Wombats
Surfing for Wayan
O'Leary, JI Terrorist Hunter

For further information go to www.southcom.com.au/~stolbert

Steve Tolbert

Dreaming Australia

Dreaming Australia
ISBN 978 1 74027 288 9
Copyright © text Steve Tolbert 2004
Cover: Mark Jolliffe

First published 2004
Reprinted 2016

GINNINDERRA PRESS
PO Box 3461 Port Adelaide 5015
www.ginninderrapress.com.au

One

Masar e-Sharif, Afghanistan, October 2001

As he stepped up out of the rubble and moved closer, Soraya stared at his black turbaned head and thickly bearded face. Seconds later, more of him showed: his black shawl, the rifle slung across his back, baggy trousers and a cable whip dangling from his hand.

A tap on the shoulder startled her before Khalida's soft voice murmured in her ear, "It's your turn to sit with the class and my turn to be spotter now."

"Sshh," Soraya cautioned, keeping her eyes fastened on the Taliban policeman until he stopped in a pool of sunlight some ten metres away. Then she pointed to the corner of the otherwise blackened window, their peephole on the outside world. "Look, Khalida."

Khalida pushed her face next to Soraya's. "Shouldn't we warn the others?" she whispered, alarmed by what she saw.

They crouched down quickly when the policeman's eyes swung their way.

"You go," Soraya whispered back, pretending to be braver than she felt. "I'll stay and see what he does." After watching her friend retreat past the spread of shoes next to the door then disappear back into the classroom, she peeked back out. The policeman's pose seemed peaceful enough – his arms folded across his chest, his squinting eyes lifted towards the sky. "Go away," Soraya mumbled to herself. "Please go away and let us stay."

She reached down and felt for her burqa – the heavy head-to-foot garment with a small mesh screen to see and breathe out of. If he took another step closer, she'd have no choice but to put it on. But she'd wait until the last possible second, because she hated the moving prison of her burqa. She had ever since the Taliban came six years earlier to steal away faces. With rifles pointed, they ordered men to grow their beards and told girls and women they were only to do housework and read the Koran. And when they left the house in burqas, it had to be in the company of their mahram – a male relative.

Soraya knew the others had their burqas on now, and that the maths and English language work on the blackboard had been replaced by lines from the Koran. They'd been well drilled by her aunt – a former schoolteacher – in doing this when Taliban policemen approached.

Moments later, she heard the girls' muted chanting in Arabic. "Allah akbar – God is great. There is no god but God. Mohammed is the messenger of God. Come to prayer. Come to salvation. Prayer is better than sleep. Allah akbar. There is no god but God. Mohammed is the messenger of God…"

Sudden shouting drowned out the chants. Soraya shot a glance out the peephole.

The policeman was gazing up, his finger pointing in the air. "Planes! Planes!" he screamed above the street noise, before running off.

She ran to the door, yanked it open and raced up the steps. Looking up, she could see four white vapour trails, like chalk lines, stretching high across the sky.

Gunfire burst out.

Seconds later, the earth shook as bombs exploded and shock waves hit from the northern edge of town.

"Soraya, get in here and put on your burqa, now!" Her aunt latched on to her and whisked her back down into the makeshift classroom.

The other girls were kneeling on straw mats with their uplifted palms extended, their voices trembling in prayer. "Allah akbar. There is no god but God and Mohammed is his prophet. May Allah always be our guide, always be our anchor. Allah akbar. There is no god but God…"

The bombing ended finally and, with their books hidden away in their burqas, the girls fled the classroom with their mahrams. Soraya, her auntie, cousin and mahram Mustafa, as usual, were the last to leave.

Out on the main road, men on bicycles and motor scooters and clattering donkey carts filled with the dead and wounded rushed past them escaping the conflict, while utility trucks crammed with Taliban fighters sped in the opposite direction towards the thick smoke and dull rumble of exploding rocket shells.

When a break came, Mustafa yelled, "Let's go!"

Her auntie grabbed her and Khalida's hands and they moved stiffly across the road, then down a dirt track past other faceless women screaming for their children, finding them and herding them indoors.

Soraya's father caught up and grasped Mustafa by the arm. "Tashakor – thank you. I can get my daughter home from here, nephew," he called out breathlessly.

"Insha'allah – may it please God," Mustafa answered, not stopping.

As they separated, more bombs struck, closer this time, shaking the ground and shooting dust and debris into the air. Soraya and her father veered right and sprinted down the lane way to their open door. No sooner were they through it than the door banged shut and Soraya's mother was smothering her in a tight embrace. The bombing got further and further away, then stopped before her mother finally released her, fingering the new lace trim on the edges of her burqa screen.

"Is this what you've learned to do at girls' school today?" she asked, a tired expression on her face.

In all the turmoil, Soraya had forgotten about that lace. "Khalida gave it to me and helped me sew it on during break time, not during lesson time, Mama."

"Yes, it would be the two of you, wouldn't it?" her mother said, in a slightly disapproving tone. "You do know what the Taliban think of such adornments, don't you?"

Soraya did. Everybody did. Beauty and fashion were against the teachings of Islam, the Taliban told the people. But a little bit of lace seemed such a small thing. "I'll keep it hidden, Mama. Honest I will. Like this." Her head flopped down as though it was mounted on a loose hinge. "See? They won't see anything," she said to her feet.

"No face, no lace," her mother mumbled. "You and Khalida, both fourteen and still so willful." She sighed and shook her head in gentle reproach. "Will it take until the two of you are married before you learn to ignore yourselves?"

Soraya kept her head dropped. "I hope not," she answered submissively, suspecting what was coming next.

"I was long-married at your age," her mother noted right on cue, "and so should you have been in better times."

Married to a man twice your age, Soraya thought, who you met in the company of a chaperone a week before your wedding day.

Placing a hand under her daughter's chin, her mother lifted Soraya's head up and eyed her through the screen. A smile flickered at the corners of her mouth. "I love you," she said, quietly and simply. "Now go take off your burqa and help me make the kabuli." While Soraya did that, she turned and moved to the opposite corner to light up the gas-ring cooker.

"See anyone outside?" her father, sitting in the chair by the door, asked her brother minutes later.

Ahmed moved to the window, stroking his wispy beard. "No, no one."

"It's your uncle Mauludeen and cousin Mustafa I'm expecting. I'm sure they will come despite the shelling, for we need to talk."

A flurry of distant rockets thudded away, then just as quickly stopped. In the past few months, their sound had become as regular as the adhan – the call to prayer – that blared now from the speaker outside. While Soraya helped her mother with the food, her father and brother knelt down and prayed.

Predictably, Mauludeen and Mustafa tapped on the door just as a lamp was being lit and small servings of kabuli – rice with sultanas and carrots – and a small pot of tea were being served up to the men. There was less food since the drought and fighting had started up again, and Soraya suspected a motive in her relatives' timely arrival.

After she escorted them through to the other room, she couldn't help saying to her mother, "They've already eaten their meals and come here now for second ones."

"Sshh." Her mother glared at her. "They are family and our guests.

Keep stirring the kabuli, I'll be right back." Minutes later, she returned with a small bag of rice and an extra measure of kerosene.

The neighbours would have to be paid back, somehow, and that irritated Soraya even more. But all she could do was hold her tongue. She took the men's food into the other room, where they sat cross-legged on the floor, the lamplight casting their upper bodies in flickering shadows on the wall. Back again, Soraya sat down and ate half of her kabuli before hopping up to collect the men's leftovers for her mother.

"Finish up all your food first before tending to the others, Soraya."

If her mother could get by with so little to eat, so could she. "I'm not hungry tonight, Mama."

Her mother's stern look silenced her. As she picked away at the rest of her kabuli, she recalled getting that same look a week earlier when, feverish and weary, her mother told her off for going out in the lane way unescorted and without her burqa on. "Get back in here!" she'd shouted then. "Oh, Soraya, why were you born so contrary, born to continually question and do such stupid things?" Seconds later, her mother's thin arms went tightly around her. "I didn't…" Something seemed to catch in her chest just where Soraya's ear was pressed. "I didn't mean to say that. I'm sorry, I'm sorry."

"It's okay, Mama."

"You're my core, my heart…" – which Soraya could hear thumping away hard in there – "…you have to know that."

"I do, Mama." Her throat started to burn. She shut her eyes against the threatening tears and willed herself to see that blackboard and the English sentences written on it earlier in the day. *This is my house, where is yours? It is across the road behind the shop. Oh, I saw it yesterday. It is a big house with many rooms.*

Her mother's breathing settled; her grip loosened. "Things will get better. You'll see… You need to eat now."

After finishing all but one mouthful of her kabuli, Soraya collected everyone's leftovers and watched her mother eat them, before helping her clean up. Another lamp was lit close to the door and they sat down to mend rips in Ahmed's tunic and robe. As usual, Soraya soon got bored. She watched her mother for a moment then reached back for her storybook hidden under the blanket. Her auntie had lent it to her. It was the story of a beautiful merchant's daughter in the 1920s during the time the great Amanullah Khan ruled Afghanistan and began to modernise the country. Soraya only had a few pages to go and was eager to finish it.

"We'll have to find you a husband who owns a library," her mother remarked, without glancing up from her sewing.

Wouldn't that be a dream, Soraya thought as she extracted her page marker from the book. Despite the many Taliban decrees about what women could and couldn't do, her mother and auntie had long encouraged her to read, as had her father, by his habit of looking the other way.

In the final chapter, the merchant's daughter married Amanullah's handsome nephew. Though the marriage was arranged, of course, the daughter and nephew had spent considerable chaperoned time together. His interest in her turned to love and that love grew to the point where he wrote her poetry every day and read it to her in the lush gardens of Amanullah's palace. The poetry professed not only his love for her but also a desire "to bathe with her in scented oils, to sprinkle her with roses and jasmine and to lie with her on their wedding night as moonbeams fell over them like water". Soraya eyed her mother and tried to visualise what all that might be like, but after a while she gave up.

Just the sporadic bark of a dog and voices that seeped through from the other room disturbed the quiet. While her mother concentrated on sewing, Soraya listened intently and caught scraps of conversation.

"The Taliban say America wants to own the world, Rahman," her uncle said, "that the world Islamic revolution is a battle between men who believe in God, praise be to Allah, and men who believe in nothing but money."

"Yes, so we are told. But people cannot be fed on religion alone, Mauludeen, as the hungry here are finding out."

"Ah yes, that is true. Life may be short, Rahman, but Allah akbar – God is great."

There was a pause before more muffled conversation followed. She heard something about the Hajj mabruk, and the cities of Kabul and Peshawar. Soraya's curiosity soared. If her mother had not been there next to her, she'd have crept closer.

Half an hour later, the mending was finished. The fuel in their lamp had run out and they were sitting there in the darkness when the men came out. After her uncle and cousin left, mattresses were rolled out without a word being spoken. Her mother and father retired to the other room and she and Ahmed to their spots on either side of the window.

"Peshawar's in Pakistan, isn't it, Ahmed?" Soraya asked as soon as he'd settled.

"Balay – yes."

"So it must be very far away."

"About four days by bus."

She knew it was probably useless, but she couldn't help muttering in her sweetest voice, "What were you talking about in there tonight?"

"Father will tell you when he wants you to know." The expected reprimanding tone wasn't there, though. The unusual softness and, yes, even affection in his voice confirmed that something big had been discussed.

She wondered if she might get away with one more question. "When do you think he'll want me to know?"

"How would I know?" he snapped back. "Go to sleep."

She drew her blanket up over her and lay there trying to draw together the few leads she had. War with America was one. There was something she'd overheard on Taliban radio weeks earlier at her auntie's place, about planes that had crashed into a building there. Had someone from Masar e-Sharif been responsible for that? Her mother said she didn't know. But it must have been so, otherwise why were they being told the Americans were responsible for dropping all the bombs and sky demons on the city? She mulled over the few words she'd picked up from the conversation. *Hajj mabruk.* Well, every Moslem knew about the blessed pilgrimage men were expected to make once in their lifetime to Mohammed's birthplace in

Mecca. Kabul was Afghanistan's capital city located over high mountains to the south-east somewhere. And she knew about Peshawar now, didn't she?

As a dogfight broke out, accompanied by a chorus of barking and howling, she thought about all this. After the dogs went quiet again, she tried one last question. "Are we going somewhere, Ahmed?"

No answer came.

Two

It was like the shrill whistling of someone high above the classroom. It strengthened to the sound of a blizzard beating down their laneway, before swooping in low and ringing their ears. Terrified, most covered them, and their eyes shot up as though the roof was made of glass.

"Get down! Get down!" her auntie shrieked, scrambling around and pushing her students into prone positions.

It roared overhead.

The spotter ran in shouting, "Sky demon! Sky demon!"

"Get down!"

The huge explosion rocked the basement, prompting screams and hurling bits of dirt and wood down on them.

Soraya leapt up and raced for the door, praying that she was wrong, that the sky demon had got beyond their neighbourhood before crashing, and that her mother would be outside their door – okay, horror-struck, but unhurt, alive and reaching out to her in gratitude and pulling her indoors. But the direction it was going and the time it took before exploding?

"Stay here!" her auntie shouted.

But Soraya was out, up the steps and streaking across the road. Brakes screeched. People screamed. No matter, her eyes stayed fixed on that great wall of smoke, grit and dust mushrooming up from where she lived.

Spilling out of doorways, men in skullcaps soon cluttered up the laneway, staring. She cut past them, her eyes running tears, her stomach sick with fear. Light dimmed suddenly as she swept around the last corner into hot, swirling smoke that covered everything in front of her. She slowed. "Mama!" She fought to breathe, to find a way through it all. "Mama!"

Others were screaming around her.

She coughed and stumbled. "Mama!" She tried to run on, but fell flat, striking her mouth and head on chunks of rubble.

An arm encircled her and dragged her back.

"No, please!" She kicked and fought. "My mother's in there! Let go! Let go!"

A second person grabbed her legs and she was bundled screaming and crying back out into the sunlight. Dropped to the ground, her head shot up. A circle of men's eyes glared down at her. Ash fell. The taste of something thick and sweet filled her mouth. She got to her knees, wiping blood away with the back of her hand and pleading with each one of those close, recognisable faces.

"Help me," she wept. "Please." In that tight space, she struggled to stand up.

"Stay there!" A policeman raised his cable whip and lashed her across the legs.

She hit the ground again, cowering and trying to crawl away. But there was no room. The more she screamed for help, the more she was lashed.

"It's all right, it's all right! I've got her burqa! I'll put it on her!" Inside her own burqa, her auntie burrowed through the crowd and reached down to get to her.

The policeman stopped and eyed her auntie with disdain, before stepping back. "Insha'allah," he quipped, breathing hard.

The burqa dropped over her. Consumed in darkness, Soraya's arms were momentarily pinned to her sides. "Noooo!" Her screams drove all but her auntie and the policeman back. "Wake me up, Auntie! Please!" Her arms escaped. Light flooded back. She flailed the air trying to get up, but was subdued by the policeman and wrapped up in her burqa again. "I want you here now, Mama! Hold me! Please, Mama! Please!"

Three

She'd heard about it at the bazaar, this open field on the city's southern fringe, where hundreds of new graves – including the twenty-eight newest ones – were marked by small piles of stones, but she was never allowed to come here, until now.

As the sun set in an apricot glow, Soraya stood bewildered between Khalida and her auntie and watched the men pray next to her mother's grave. Other men, she recognised, were out here kneeling in prayer as well, while their burqa-clad women stood like dark beacons behind them. Feeling disembodied, Soraya welcomed having her burqa on. It reduced life, screening her turmoil, muting the grief of nearby families and the fighting from the other side of the city. For the past five days – the time it took to unearth what was left of her mother and bury her – she'd welcomed it. Though the only times she'd left her auntie's house were when they went to the bazaar, and later to the magnificent blue mosque – site of the tomb of Ali, son-in-law of the prophet Mohammed – where for centuries Moslems from everywhere had come to pray for miracles.

In the winding bazaar – where policemen roamed like wolves – what her eyes concentrated on were not the things being sold, but on women being whipped for appearing immodest, or laughing in public, or wearing something white, or lingering too long in one spot. During quiet periods, she gazed at the severed, fly-blown hands and feet of thieves and at women's nail-polished fingers strung up alongside stalls offering rotting vegetables, shoe-shines, used clothing and odd shoes for one-legged people.

At the blue mosque – amazingly untouched by the fighting, and still surrounded by white doves and red tulips like a painting of paradise – they passed the giant Koran on a lectern, and walked over pale blue marble, smooth as glass, before separating from the men and entering the women's area. Soraya prostrated herself next to her auntie and cousin and prayed to Allah for her own miracle, that of being reunited with her mother in a place of eternal peace.

Dust floated in the dull twilight now. Her upper lip itched, so she rubbed her tongue back and forth across it and glanced over at the entry gate. A white Taliban flag, inscribed in black Koranic verse – "There is no God but Allah and Mohammed is his messenger" – fluttered away there. Above the main road, where kites used to fly and kite runners used to run, only crows circled now. Further on, despite the failing light, the blue mosque's huge dome and minaret stood out like a great spiked eye above the rooftops.

Her head started to ache. It tended to after she'd been standing for a long time. The lumped bruise on her cheekbone and the taped, swollen gash along her upper lip she'd have carried with some pride in earlier days. How often her mother had smiled down at her and said with feigned concern, "There are times, Soraya, when I think you should have been born a boy – born a boy – born a boy – born a boy." Her voice echoed, refusing to go away.

When Mustafa joined them, her auntie took their hands. Following Mustafa, she led them out of the grave field, back along the busy main road and down an alleyway past the new masses of rubble that had once been Soraya's home and neighbourhood.

Her auntie's place was larger than Soraya's had been, with three rooms instead of two. Mauludeen – a merchant like her father – had once had two wives, so a ladder had been made and a second bedroom built over the first. But his second wife got sick and died just after the Taliban came. So there was room enough for the three of them up there now.

When her father, uncle and Ahmed returned that evening, the men sat on a threadbare carpet in an adjoining room and smoked pipes and talked, more out of habit than desire, until her father divulged his changed plans to them. Voices lowered and quickened then. Though, if Soraya had been interested, she still might have overheard what was being said. She wasn't, so she didn't.

After the meal and the cleaning up, she excused herself in order to pass through to the ladder and go to bed.

But her father had other ideas. He pointed to the space next to him. "Sit down, daughter," he instructed. "There are matters to discuss which you need to know about." After she sat, he placed a hand over hers and stared at the burning lamp on the floor. "Fighting," he said, using his other hand to rub his long, grey-flecked beard. "It has been the enemy of our country for three decades now, so that our children have never known the security of peace: fighting with the Russians, fighting with the Taliban from the south, and always fighting with our tribal selves spurred on by power-hungry warlords who measure honour by their ability to exact revenge. And now, of all people, the Americans have come to unleash their firepower from the sky. Always the fighting and suffering and death. Afghanistan's gone insane." He eyed his daughter and smiled weakly at her. "A year ago, we paid the price poorer fathers could not pay to keep our sons out of the Taliban army. But despite what their radio stations tell us, Taliban deaths have been high lately. Soon they will come again for our sons and this time they will say, 'We need fighters, not money', and they won't accept any bribe below a king's fortune. And once again there will be no winners for us whatever happens. We, as Pashtun people, were treated badly by the Northern Alliance when last they ruled here. So there's no reason to think things will be any different should they defeat the Taliban and reoccupy the city."

"True, brother. It's like choosing between the jackal and the snake," Mauludeen pitched in.

"Though I'd prefer the Northern Alliance jackal to the Taliban snake," Ahmed ventured, quietly. "At least they didn't deprive of us of our basic freedoms and customs."

"Perhaps," Rahman replied, rubbing his eyes with thumb and finger and dropping his head momentarily. "Anyway, you'll recall that before my home was destroyed and my wife sent to her grave, I'd discussed thoughts about not taking my hajj mabruk."

"I do, brother," Mauludeen said, puffing on his pipe and greasing his beard with a mutton bone. "How quickly our joy and sadness become sisters. Hajj mabruk, the dream of a man's lifetime, more meaningful than even birth or death."

Her father nodded and continued, "Instead of going to Mecca, my idea was to use the money I'd save to flee to Pakistan and start a new life there. You, Mustafa, with your knowledge of the mountains and provinces to the east, said you would lead us to the border."

"Balay."

"And once we were settled, you and your family, Mauludeen, would consider selling up and coming to Pakistan also."

"Balay."

"Now there is much turmoil in that country too, as firebrand Pakistanis join the call for jihad. It's no longer a safe place for my children to start new lives. They must go beyond Pakistan." He turned towards Soraya. "You're sitting here now to learn about a journey you're about to take with your brother and nephew, and to learn also what you're to do if anything bad should happen to them."

"But, Father, I don't want…"

"Shush!" he said sharply, lifting his hand from hers. "Arrangements have been made. It is for the best. Insha'allah."

Her spirit wilted under his heavy eyes, her head dropped. One minute affectionate, the next he was so stern with her. She felt like burying herself in her burqa and hiding away in a corner. But she could only sit there and listen in chastened silence.

"Tomorrow, Ahmed, Mustafa and you will board a bus and leave Masar e-Sharif."

"But how can that be?" Soraya blurted out. "Women can't travel on…"

"Sshhh. Just listen to me! That bus will get you as far as Kabul. There you will board another. When you get close to the Pakistan border, you will get off the bus. Mustafa knows a route across a loosely guarded section of the border and he will lead you over it as far as a bazaar in the city of Peshawar. There you will meet a man by the name of Pervez Lateef. He will organise the rest of your journey."

The rest of the journey to where, Soraya wanted to ask before her uncle spoke up again.

"It will be a hard journey, a man's journey, will it not, Rahman?"

"Ah, yes, tashakor, Brother. It certainly will be. Buses break down. Blizzards can block the roads this time of year. So you'll have to be prepared for the worst. You will wear strong boots and carry adequate provisions in case you need to walk some of the way. And Soraya," he said, looking back down at her, "you will leave your burqa here."

"Why? How can…"

He looked sternly down his beard at her again. "Tonight your aunt will cut your hair. Tomorrow, along with boots, you will wear loose trousers, a woollen scarf around your face and a thick tunic and robe. You will also wrap your head in a turban."

"Am I to travel as a boy, then?"

"It is not unheard of lately and it will be safer." His eyes lingered on her, turning softer in the lamplight. "Your mother used to say that you should have been born a boy."

Tears welled up. "I know."

He covered her hand with his again. "So now you must demonstrate how right she could be, Soraya, and do your family proud. Once you get to Pakistan, you may become our daughter again."

She acknowledged all this with a dumbfounded nod. "After Pakistan, the rest of the journey will be to where, Father?" she asked quietly.

"I've a cousin in the rich country of Australia. He shares our family name. Hamid Khan Zadran lives in a place called Penrith, close to the big city of Sydney. I've written to him and given Ahmed his address. You're to go there."

She was never going to wake up. "Australia must be very far away."

"Balay."

Pipes and the hissing lamp occupied their attention.

"What language do they speak, Father?"

"English."

"That's good, anyway," Soraya muttered dismally.

"You will need to put your English language book and dictionary into your pack. You're to continue studying the language at every opportunity."

"You will be coming to Australia soon, Father?"

"When there is again enough money. Insha'allah."

"Promise, Father?" she asked meekly.

He turned his attention to her auntie standing at the doorway, before motioning for both of them to leave.

*

"It's only for a brief time and it will grow back quickly," her auntie said, snipping away at her hair as she sat slumped on a stool in Mustafa's loose clothes. "And do you know, Soraya, before the Taliban came, I saw photos of Australia women in magazines. I can remember them clearly. Their hair was short, not much longer than men's, so by the time you get there, your hair won't be any shorter than theirs. Though…" She paused and clicked her tongue disapprovingly. Her voice dropped. "Though you should know other things in those photos were short too, like their dresses – when they wore them – and tiny tops that barely covered their breasts, and…and I want you to promise me you'll never go swimming in the ocean there."

Soraya's wall of silence cracked. "All right, but why not, Auntie?"

"Because, my beautiful niece, men and women only wear underwear…" – hair cutting stopped as she bent over to whisper in Soraya's ear – "…no bigger than period belts to swim in. Which reminds me. When are you due to start your period again?"

How ridiculous, Soraya thought. Becoming a boy and talking periods. She shrugged and stared at her hair on the floor. "In a few days, I think."

"You need to know that your belt and pads are next to your underwear at the very bottom of your pack." She stood up straight again.

"Tashakor, Auntie."

"You're welcome, Abdul."

"What?"

"Exhale. Leave only enough air in your lungs to thank me again."

"Tashakor, Auntie." Her voice was deeper this time.

"Good. Now, while travelling to Pakistan, you will be Abdul, and Ahmed and Mustafa will do all the talking for you when they can but, if you're forced to say something, keep your head dropped, your breath out, and tense the muscles in your throat and stomach before you do. Let's practise. What's your name?"

"Abdul."

"Where do you live, Abdul?"

"Masar e-Sharif."

"Why are you going to Pakistan?"

"To visit a brother who is working in Peshawar."

"Good. When next I see a photo from Australia, I expect it will be of you making a movie there, or acting on the stage, for you are a truly talented girl."

"As Abdul," Soraya added in her new voice, keeping her head down and willing her eyes to stay dry.

Her auntie laughed. "As my only niece who I will miss every minute of every day."

*

She'd never been in a bus, or ever out of eyesight of Masar e-Sharif before. As the chaos of men jostling for space inside and on the roof of the chugging, smoke-belching bus continued, Soraya longed for the anonymity of her burqa – its thick, sound-muffling fabric, its small screen of reality. The outside world would soon be too big, too close and threatening without it. After her hair was cut and she'd gone to bed, she'd wept silently and fretted so much in the night that, by the time the muezzin's call to prayer sounded, there was nothing left inside her but a weary calm. That weariness and her puffy eyes remained, but the calm was gone, replaced now by a fear of what lay ahead and a loneliness that already surged through her like an electric current.

While her auntie chatted to her about little things, the men gripped their sons' shoulders, pressed their cheeks to their sons' cheeks and sent them on their way. After Ahmed departed, Rahman came over to her. Looking up into his glassy eyes, she knew then that, yes, he could grieve, and what she wanted to do was reach up and wrap her arms tightly around him, burying her face in his beard. But she couldn't. Her father adjusted the scarf around her face, so only her eyes were visible, then held her by the arms. "Time to go." He suddenly sounded a long way off. "Ahmed and Mustafa are saving you a place at the back of the bus."

This was it, the end of what remained of her life in Masar e-Sharif. She could barely shift her eyes in the direction of the bus, Perhaps, she thought, the bus would break down, or she could get off at the first stop, evade Ahmed and Mustafa and make her way back, somehow.

"Be careful and be wary," Rahman said. "Never trust fat men in poor places. Stick close to your brother and cousin. Remember Hamid Khan Zadran. I've written his address on the inside cover of your English book. We will one day meet you there. Insha'allah." He placed her pack in her hands. "Above all else, bring honour to our family and your mother's memory." With that, her father pressed a hand to her back, as though a handle were there, and moved her towards the bus.

Soraya tightened her woollen shawl and she stepped nervously onto the men's bus. Almost everyone had belongings, bundled up in blankets, wedged in the spaces below them or were sitting on them in the aisle. She shuffled past people and property, accidentally kicking an old man and apologising in her deepest Abdul voice. At the back, she squeezed past Ahmed and Mustafa, sat in the window seat and looked out between dangling legs at her father and uncle, her auntie and Khalida. The bus revved its engine. Gears crunched. As they shot forward, she gave a quick wave, wondering if she would see any of them again. Only the women waved back.

Down the main road they went and soon they were on the city's outskirts, rocking and jolting past the field of graves. Newer ones extended down the row her mother was buried in. Tears welled up again. Holding her scarf in place, she stuck her head out the window and looked back at the graves and Masar e-Sharif disappearing in a haze of dusty light.

Four

The bus rumbled on, leaning sharply into turns, gearing down, inching up inclines and speeding downhill again.

After a while, a couple of passengers bowed their heads out of windows and bellowed sickly warnings. When the smell of vomit joined the odour of musty clothes, exhaust and diesel fuel, Soraya grew nauseous and tried unsuccessfully to lose herself in daydreams. She got out her English book and started to read a passage about a dog that rescued people from an avalanche, but that only made her feel worse.

"Put the book away and keep your eyes on where we're going," Mustafa called out when she dropped her head in her hands.

Soraya obeyed. She found a section of window clear of stains, legs and feet and tried to read her future out there in the desolate landscape and huge, metallic sky. It did little to stem her gloom, though, as the only things capable of movement in that wasteland were the breeze-struck branches of a few dead trees and willy-willies that blew up and shifted dirt on the horizon. "There's never been a drought like this one. Year by year, the desert draws closer to Masar e-Sharif. We don't need continual war to ensure starvation. The drought can do that by itself," she recalled her father saying to Mustafa one night.

Later, the landscape darkened. Signs of habitation showed – neglected almond trees, withering vines and the skeletons of vehicles along the side of the road. Stooped farmers worked the few parched fields still in use. Along village tracks, donkeys and camels transported wood. Women in burqas toted water jugs and washing buckets on their heads from wells that still held water. Taliban fighters in open trucks – their long robes flapping behind them – regularly passed heading in the opposite direction. The bus slowed once, passing a pock-marked field, its irrigation channels demolished and dry. Buzzards circled the burnt-out remains of a tractor. What was once a village was now a ruin of craters and splintered beams jutting from mounds of mud brick and stone. Neither people nor animals moved. Further along, small flags fluttered over the graves of the recent dead.

As tears came again, Soraya curtained her face with her shawl. Her father's words came to her. *Above all else, bring honour to your family and memory of your mother.* No, she wouldn't be getting off and going back. She wiped her eyes and stared back out the window as the bus bounced over the potholed road that often seemed rougher than the land itself. In Australia, the people speak English, she remembered. "Good morning," she whispered to herself. "My name is Soraya. I come from Masar e-Sharif in Afghanistan. What's your name? Oh, that is a nice name. How are you? I am fine too. What is your religion? I am a Moslem. What do you like to do? I like to read books and…and fifty-seven and forty-eight is one hundred and five. I am good doing mathematics. What are you good doing?"

Men chatted, dozed, were tossed awake and dozed off again in front of her. A few continued to groan, still sick and senseless.

Approaching a series of small villages, the driver beeped his horn and the bus shuddered to a stop. A few got off. Ragged boys squatting next to roofless buildings and broken walls got up and trotted over yelling and waving. Bony dogs followed. The boys lifted their palms to the open windows begging for coins. "Baksheesh, baksheesh," they pleaded, before the bus moved off. Immersed in road dust and exhaust, the dogs raced after the bus, snapping at the tyres to chase them away.

Brown hills showed on the horizon and grew taller until the bus climbed into them. In the early afternoon, they arrived at Aybak and stopped across from a bazaar roofed in animal hides. Above the entryway was a banner that read, "AMERICA, THE ENEMY OF HUMANITY". Below it, dogs slept, while gaunt-faced amputees, war widows and a blind man sat cross-legged on the ground, their begging bowls in front of them.

After Mustafa volunteered to guard their seats, Ahmed and Soraya joined passengers streaming out the door and off the roof. Across the road, they dropped coins in bowls and entered the bazaar, passing tea drinkers grouped around tightly packed stalls, old men squatting beside pyramids of withered fruit, and kebab sellers fanning smoky braziers of meat. Here too, hands were roped to a branch of a solitary tree.

In an open area behind the last tea stall, Ahmed spotted a dilapidated mud-brick enclosure. Men went in and out of it. "I'll just use the toilet, then we can go buy some food," he mentioned to Soraya.

"But Ahmed…"

"And don't go anywhere, brother," he interjected loudly, scowling and moving closer. "You're Abdul, remember?" he said in a low voice.

Soraya grabbed his arm and adjusted her voice. "Sorry. But I have to go to the same place you do."

His eyes rolled in their sockets. "Can't you just wait until the next town?"

"No. Can you?"

He groaned. "Well, there's an open field running off the end of the bazaar."

"You use it, then. I'm not."

"Nobody will watch."

She had to allow herself to be guided by him in most things, but not this. "No."

His lips tightened. He shook his head in frustration before glancing at the enclosure and thinking for a moment. "All right. Stay here until I get back."

"You better hurry."

He did, and when he returned, he said, "Okay, this is what you do. Hold your stomach and drop your head… That's it. Now picture those people being sick on the bus and what stuck to the window and what flew past it. And the sounds. 'Aaaaahhh'," he mimicked softly. "Remember them? Now do what they did. Gag. Go on, do it! That's right." He led her quickly over to the enclosure. "Go in and keep gagging, but louder. I'll stop people at the entrance."

Half a minute in there and she no longer had to pretend. After she came out, there was only one man waiting next to Ahmed. He wore a black turban and baggy trousers. A rifle was strapped to his back and he carried a cable whip. The shock of him stopped her in her tracks.

A slow frown gathered on the policeman's forehead as his black-eyed glare bore into her. "You're not well?"

Her face flushed in panic. She looked down at her hands in respect and shook her head.

"A pity." He scrutinised her from head to foot. "But then, at least you have the money to buy the scarce food that you can vomit back up in the toilets." He paused, staring at her. "You are not from Aybak, are you?"

Soraya felt herself trembling. She made a point of rubbing her mouth with the shawl, before shaking her head again.

"So where do you live?"

"My brother and I live in Masar e-Sharif," Ahmed blurted out. "We're on our way to Kabul to visit our uncle. Insha'allah."

The policeman glared at Ahmed now. "You are brave boys to be making such a journey when the Americans are dropping so many bombs everywhere. But perhaps you are men now. If so, you should be fighting with the Taliban army. How old are you?"

"Fourteen," Ahmed lied.

The policeman swung his eyes back Soraya's way. "And you?"

"My brother's twelve," Ahmed said quickly.

He glared at Ahmed again. "Tell me, does your brother have a tongue, or has it been cut out of his head?"

"Balay… Um, I mean he does have one, balay."

"Then…"

A plane roared overhead. Gunfire rattled the air. The policeman bolted for the enclosure, as others dashed for the walls.

Ahmed pushed Soraya hard in the back. "Let's go!"

By the time they got back to the bus, people were on their feet again dropping coins, fanning coals and sipping glasses of tea as if nothing unusual had happened.

"Ahmed," Mustafa called out from the roof of the bus.

They looked up to see Mustafa kneeling next to their bags. He lifted his palms in the air, shrugged and pointed down to where they had been sitting. Through the open window were two Taliban fighters. Propped in front of them, the barrel of a rocket launcher pointed upwards as if it were about to blow off the roof.

Mustafa moved to the ladder and climbed down. "Sorry."

"Don't be silly. There's nothing you could have done."

"No. Did you get food?"

"Not yet."

They scanned the open windows. The driver and many of the passengers hadn't returned.

Ahmed glanced back at the bazaar. The policeman was strolling through the animals and people towards them. "Right then," he said quickly. "First we feed our souls, then our stomachs. Insha'allah." He pointed to a small mosque next to the bazaar.

Inside the mosque, they could just make out a straw-covered floor and a lamp burning in a niche of the wall. Facing that wall, and using their robes as prayer mats, men knelt down and pressed their foreheads to the ground, then lifted them and extended their palms upwards.

Soraya found Abdul's voice. "I'll meet you here, then."

"You have to come with us," Ahmed said, keeping his eye on the policeman.

Her voice turned low. "Men worship apart from women."

"Don't look around, Abdul," Ahmed warned her, "because the policeman who questioned us is coming our way." Again his hand pressed against her back, moving her on.

Despite his best intentions, Ahmed playing their father was beginning to irritate Soraya.

"This is our prayer, Abdul. O mighty Allah," Ahmed chanted. "This mosque is your mosque. This peace is your peace. This slave is your slave…"

"I know it," Soraya said tersely. "I'm not a child."

Tat – tat – tat – tat – tat – tat – tat… Gunfire burst out. Running across the road, they looked up to see three vapour trails moving southwards towards Kabul.

*

Huddled up against the mountain cold an hour out of Aybak, it was Mustafa who first spotted the Taliban fighters. "Get down!" he screamed. "Hold on!"

Roof riders went flat, grabbing at the handrails, as the bus screeched and skidded in the gravel. Bags spilled off and passengers shouted as the bus pitched towards a crevasse looming up like a deep scar on their right. They smashed into a boulder, crunching metal, before pulling up short of the edge. No one moved, nothing was said. Only the clanks and knocks of the engine and a wind gust could be heard before a few fighters split from the Taliban group and began running in opposite directions along the road.

Their officer – a sleek-bearded man wearing a turban and bandoliers of bullets criss-crossing his chest – shouted out, "Let nothing through until we're finished here!" With that, he and others approached, encircling the bus and brandishing their weapons. "Everyone off the bus!" he ordered.

"Don't say a word," Ahmed told Soraya, working the worry beads around his neck.

Once they were in line with the other passengers on the opposite side of the road, more fighters and supply-carrying porters appeared and moved towards the bus.

While the officer interrogated the driver, Mustafa mumbled frantically, "If we're separated, remember Pervez Lateef's Rugs, Khyber Bazaar, Peshawar."

"Hamid Khan Zadran too, in Penrith," Ahmed added, "near Sydney, Australia."

The driver was sent back to his bus, while others were told to sit down or sent to carry supplies.

28

Eventually, the officer got down to them. Thick eyebrows overhung deep-set eyes that drilled into them. "You're together?"

Mustafa answered, "Balay."

"Brothers?"

Mustafa tapped his chest. "Cousin," then pointed to the others. "They're brothers."

"Who's the oldest?"

"I am," Ahmed said before Mustafa could.

The officer fronted Ahmed. "You're a porter now. Get down the road and help out."

Ahmed swung around blindly and left them.

"You two sit. You're not to move until the bus is gone. When it is, pick up your things and walk back to where you came from."

"But…"

"The officer scowled at Mustafa and moved a step closer. "You're not happy with that?"

"Balay. But…"

"But, but!" the officer shouted. "Get it out!"

"You see, we were sent to Kabul by our father, who stayed in Masar e-Sharif to help Taliban forces defend the town."

The officer's face softened a little. "Kabul will soon be under attack like Masar e-Sharif is. Your brother will be there by tomorrow to help us defeat our enemies. To join him, you can follow him now. Otherwise…" He pointed to the ground.

Soraya sat down first, followed by Mustafa.

The officer left.

*

Soraya sat there listening to the stray sounds: the bus climbing the road above them and the muted voices and gravel-crunching footsteps of those retrieving their things. Her first movement was to draw her knees up, lay her forehead on them and replay more familiar sounds in her head: the voice of her mother, rice boiling, the hiss of the stove and the lamp at night. As her reverie strengthened, her shawl fell away in the wind.

The sound of their bags plopping down brought her mind back. "People will recognise you," Mustafa said, wrapping the shawl back around her.

"What does it matter?" she said, no longer caring to play Abdul.

"It matters a lot," Mustafa replied close to her ear. "Passengers are angry and could take their frustrations out on you. There could be more Taliban around. A truck or another bus might come. Remember what your father said: until we get to Pakistan, you're safer being a boy." He sat down beside her again. "And what about bringing honour to the family and the memory of your mother? You can't do that by giving up now." When she showed her surprise, he explained, "Your father has never been known for his quiet voice."

"No."

"You must know, Soraya, there aren't many families in Afghanistan who would pay for their daughters to be taken to another country."

"I know."

He looked straight into her red raw eyes. "Then you tell me what you think we should do."

Five

"Do you know where you're to go?"

It was as though someone had emerged from a cut in the rocks, for they thought all the passengers had gone. Jerking their heads around, they saw an old man with a beak-like nose and long, white beard. From under his flat pakol cap, hair streamed down to partially cover his worn backpack.

"To Kabul, or at least in the general direction of the place. Insha'allah," Mustafa answered.

The old man's quick laugh was like a cough. "Then I'd make the direction as general as possible. For it seems our capital is once again turning into a war zone." He leaned heavily on a walking stick and stared impassively at them for a moment, before a grin lifted his cracked cheeks. "I live in the mountains north of Kabul, about two days' walk from here." He turned on his heel and started moving away. "I wouldn't object to your company if you'd like to follow along. At least I should be able to keep you from stepping on a landmine. Insha'allah. Is there a more Afghan way of dying nowadays?" He appeared to be asking himself the question.

They grabbed their things and quickly caught up with him.

"My name's Muhammed," the old man said, looking around at them and scratching his beard.

"I'm Mustafa, and this is my cousin, Abdul."

"Abdul? What an interesting name for a girl."

Mustafa and Soraya exchanged glances, nothing more.

Though he was soon puffing, the old man maintained a steady pace in front of them. When heavy vehicles got close, they ducked in behind boulders. Every passing vehicle carried fighters towards Kabul.

"I'd rather be around a bear than those Taliban with all their weapons," the old man said, shaking his head. "When you're Taliban, your only interest is destroying what you never learned how to build."

On up they went into the boulder-grey world, past running snowmelt, the residue of rockslides and the deepening gorge below. Wind whipped grit into their faces. Air thinned and got even colder when the sun dropped and shadows moved over them. Their quick breath misted and faded, misted and faded. Sleeves of snow began to show and lengthen and thicken.

When the old man stopped at a hairpin turn, he scooped up a handful of snow and put it in his mouth. Thirst quenched, he glanced to his left. "My way's that way. If you haven't changed your mind, you're still free to follow along. But if you do, remember please, there are mines buried in the ground and others that look like toy dolls above it. So watch where you put your hands as well as your feet. Don't wander, just follow in my footsteps."

They had to look hard to see the stone track that wound steeply up between two massive boulder walls.

"Just another hour, then we can stop for the night," the old man added, setting off with determined strides.

*

Under the rock overhang, Muhammed used a foot to smooth out the remains of a camp fire. He dropped sticks, thorny branches and dried dung between it and their snow-filled cooking pots. "Manda nabashi," he said, out of the blue.

"What?" Mustafa asked, mystified, after he and Soraya deposited their collection of fuel as well.

"Manda nabashi," Muhammed repeated, slapping his hands together for warmth. He peered out at a snow-topped peak gleaming under the sinking sun. "May you not be tired. It's the normal greeting in these mountains. You will hear it spoken often. To reply, just say 'Zanda bashi – may you continue to live well.'" He bent down, rummaged through his pack and took out some paper, matches and a tattered robe. "Local greetings will be good to know when you want to soften up the fighters you'll meet along the way." He passed the paper and matches over to Soraya with that little grin showing again. "Would you please light the fire?"

"Balay," she answered, starting to shiver in the cold.

"Tashakor. Zanda bashi." He turned to Mustafa. "Now that that's being taken care of, come along with me and we'll look at the wheat crop." He took befuddled Mustafa by the arm and led him down the track.

Soraya had the fire lit and the cooking pots on by the time they returned. At the edge of the low campfire light, they laid out their robes before the men knelt down and faced the sunset for namaz – evening prayer.

"Will you be joining us? You're welcome to," Muhammed asked Soraya, smiling into her eyes.

"No. I'll pray alone later," she answered, pleased she could be herself again without fear of retribution, at least for now.

Once the food had been cooked and served up, they sat cross-legged by the fire and ate their rice, naan bread and goat's cheese without disturbing the mountain silence. After prayers, Soraya and Mustafa folded up turbans and placed them on stones for pillows, then wrapped themselves up in robes and blankets and lay down.

In minutes, Mustafa was asleep, but not Soraya. Ahmed prevented her. She couldn't clear her mind of him. Was he thinking about them as well now? Was he next to a fire too? Had he eaten? Certainly he'd have no one like Muhammed close by. She tried to picture what the next few days would be like for him: the chaos and fighting, streets filled with the wounded and dead. Her mind flashed back. *Get down! Get down!* That great roar shaking the classroom. *Sky demon! Sky demon!* She curled up into a ball then and prayed a second time, silently.

The old man drank tea, periodically glancing over at Soraya. She was far too young to be struggling for sleep, he thought. But war did that to people, regardless of their age. When her breathing finally did grow heavy, he turned his attention to the stars that fanned out overhead. Soon those stars faded as a full moon – like the heart of the sky – pressed up and splashed the mountains in moonlight. In this interlude, with the extraordinary universe on show, fixed in eternal silence, time vanished. "Stillness is beauty," Muhammed reminded himself, eyeing the heavens. He felt close again and was grateful. "Allah akbar." Pictures of his smiling wife and daughter occupied his mind, as they often did this time of night. He added more branches and dung to the fire then looked over at his companions. "May Allah be your guide and your anchor wherever in this world you're allowed to find peace," he mumbled to them, as he had to others here over the years.

After a while, Muhammed got to his feet and walked up to a spot overlooking a valley. Pinpricks of yellow light twinkled against the darkness down there. Some were the campfires of fighters, others of those fleeing the fighting. His nostalgia grew. In the distant past, you'd rarely see the light of a single fire in this valley, rarely hear anything but the rain and wind, the rumble and crack of a passing storm. But these mountains were no longer what they were. And from what he'd seen and heard, during his short stay in Masar e-Sharif, he knew things were only going to get worse. But where else could he go? Devoting himself to god up here, he'd always thought, allowed him to exist without having to participate in earthly affairs any more. "But it seems no matter how far you go alone into the wilderness," he mumbled to himself, "you can't completely shut your eyes against the visible world: people suffering and dying, the starvation of hope."

*

Soraya woke up rigid in the early morning light. It took her a moment to feel the aches in her body and connect them with the rocks, smoke and ash to work out where she was.

The fire was going. The old man sat cross-legged boiling up tea and looking serene.

Watching him, she recalled stories her mother told her about spiritual men who lived by themselves in the mountains. What were they called? "Rohani," she uttered aloud, not meaning to. When he flicked his eyes her way, she stuttered, "Um. I mean good morning."

The old man scratched his beard, grinning. "And good morning to you, Abdul."

"Soraya."

"No, Muhammed."

"I mean my real name is Soraya," she said, a twinkle in her voice.

"Ah yes, Soraya. Sorry. An old man's hearing has a tendency to break down occasionally. And tell me, Soraya, how do you know about rohani?"

She told him.

The fire held his gaze for a moment, before he replied. "I think sometimes I'd starve inside if I were not such a person." He looked up at her again. "Anyway, it sounds like your mother's a very knowledgeable woman."

Soraya lowered her eyes. "Yes, she was."

They stared into the fire until Mustafa stirred and greeted them in a sleepy voice.

Muhammed reached into his pack for food and utensils. "Tea's about ready." As he sliced naan bread and scooped out lumps of yoghurt onto plates, it started again – the distant thuds of artillery shells.

"Kabul?" Mustafa asked incredulously.

The old man listened hard. "It seems so. Few would have believed the fighting could have spread there so quickly." He poured tea into metal glasses and passed them around. "Don't be concerned. Sounds travel far in these mountains."

They held their tea like offerings in their hands and blew into it, then sipped and slurped. Steam and their frosted breath merged, billowing around their faces in the icy air.

Another sound came, softly at first. Fut – fut – fut – fut – fut... It got closer and strengthened.

Muhammed set his glass down and got up. "Come with me, please. I may need your young eyes."

By the time they reached the lookout point, the drumming of rotor blades filled the valley. Mustafa spotted the helicopter – like a bloated dragonfly – emerge from a veil of morning mist.

Gunfire sounded. The helicopter swerved, dipped its nose and fired rockets that streaked to the valley floor. Puffs of smoke showed before explosions reverberated up the valley. A jet plane howled overhead, the thunder of its engines punctuating the tat – tat – tat – tat – tat of the helicopter's guns raking the ground.

Soraya shut her eyes and sobbed quietly behind them. Seconds later, she dropped to her knees and wrapped her head in her arms.

Booom! A muffled explosion jerked the men's eyes to their right.

"A mine," Muhammed shouted, barely able to be heard over the rotor blades, gunfire and jets that roamed the sky.

Whoosh! Whoosh! More rockets slammed into the valley floor. Boom! Another mine detonated.

"Aaaaaahh!" Soraya screamed wildly over the din of engines and rotor blades, rockets, guns and mines.

Six

"Sorry."

"No need to be," Muhammed replied, squatting next to her by the fire. "Others were screaming as well. We just couldn't hear them."

Since the fighting and her screaming had stopped, the mountains had grown so still that they could hear voices and hoofs passing by for minutes at a time.

"Can we just stay here a little while longer?" Soraya asked, still shaken.

"With so many fleeing along the track now, I think that would be wise."

Muhammed and Mustafa returned to the lookout point and scanned the valley. Sunlight and shadow chased each other down there. Plumes of smoke drifted away in the wind. Tiny figures could be seen on the undulating track to their right.

Feeling an explanation was needed, Mustafa told the old man about Soraya's mother and her father's efforts to get her and Ahmed out of the country.

"And Ahmed was one of those taken away yesterday?"

"Yes."

Minutes passed before the clack, clack, clack of more hoofs on rock approached.

"Time to get Soraya and go," the old man said.

They followed the switchbacks along the side of the valley as groups of Taliban fighters hurried past – the legs of their supply horses battered and bleeding.

"They treat their animals the way they do the people," Muhammed couldn't help remarking.

Unlike the Taliban fighters, villagers slowed and shot glances of recognition at Muhammed. "Manda nabashi," they said.

"Zanda bashi."

As the wind strengthened and swollen snow clouds blew over, they descended the eroded track and loose scree to the valley below. There they stopped next to a river that ran grey and fast over stones.

Muhammed eyed Soraya. "There is no other way we can go," he warned, "but through the village that was attacked this morning. You need to be ready for that."

By midafternoon, they entered the blackened, smouldering village. The acrid smell of explosives and smoke still hung heavy in the air. A trio of elders wandered through the debris pointing and mumbling, while other villagers sat slumped on the ground.

Concerned about Soraya's response, Muhammed moved quickly past the charred remains and splintered trees, the dead goats and three blanket-covered bodies. A mangy dog that bared its fangs and growled at them was all that registered their presence.

The track rose back up the valley wall. Breathing heavily, Muhammed only spoke to warn them to stay close. By the time the track flattened out again, rain and sleet had thickened to snow and darkness was closing in.

"Not long now," the old man noted.

Minutes later, they entered a narrow corridor between massive boulders and climbed to a spot open to the wind and snow.

"This way," he directed quickly.

At the end of the V-shaped corridor was a low stone hut that backed onto a huge boulder. It had a wood-plank door and a single plastic window. A stone chimney poked out of the tilted, sheet metal roof. Tin buckets collected water on the run off side. Firewood and drying dung were stacked and covered in plastic sheeting on the other.

"Welcome," Muhammed said, escorting them into the musty darkness. "This storm will pass," he said with a grin. "And though there will be other storms, within this room there will always be peace. Allah akbar." He lit a lamp hanging from a hook on the blanket-insulated ceiling.

Yellow light glowed and spread. They stood on an earthen floor with the blackened hearth and a mound of wood on their left. A scrappy curtain covered the window. Rock ledges served as bench space for books and the Koran, food and other essentials. On the floor at the back was Muhammed's bed – a rolled-up strip of foam and a small cushion. With the door shut and their packs dropped, there was just enough room for the three of them.

The old man found some matches and looked over at Soraya with a glint in his eyes. "Can you light a hearth as well as you can light a campfire?"

She was cold and tired and could feel her blisters leaking into her socks. But given their circumstances, they couldn't wish for a better place or a better person to be with. "Watch me." Tending to the fire and food was what she and her mother did in the evenings. Spotting water in a nearby pot, she added, "And you can watch me cook on it also."

"Good, good." He handed her the matches, then turned to Mustafa. "That being so, come with me, good soul, and let's check on that wheat crop."

This time Mustafa knew what to expect.

The storm continued all night. Water dripped and lumps of snow fell off the roof.

After breakfast the next morning, Muhammed showed them a basket of gemstones and explained how he made them into jewellery to sell at bazaars. Though under Taliban rule the demand for jewellery had suffered greatly, there were still a few merchants around who were prepared to buy them at a cheap price and horde them until Taliban rule ended, whenever that would be.

There were lots of discoloured storybooks and a battered English book to read. When Soraya took out her own English book and started pronouncing words from the fourth chapter, Muhammed looked over at her.

"Hello. My name is Muhammed and I live in the mountains," he said in perfect English.

His grin reminded Soraya of a small boy's after he'd been told how clever he was.

"What's your name, and where do you live, and how long have you lived there?" he asked.

Once Soraya answered all that, Muhammed explained that he'd studied the language long ago in Kabul. "Where do you live, Mustafa?" the old man went on.

Mustafa looked up from the Koran. Anxious to show what he could do, he lifted his chin and pulled his shoulders back. After answering the question, he mentioned where some of his friends and relatives lived and gave their ages.

"Excellent!" Muhammed moved closer to him. "Have you studied English in England?

"No, just in Masar e-Sharif." Sporting a proud smirk, Mustafa continued, "But before the Taliban came, I had a teacher who lived in that country."

"Well, it shows."

Soraya continued practising. "I am fourteen years old. How old are you, Mustafa?"

"I am sixteen, but I will soon be seventeen."

"And I am…" Muhammed paused, "fifty-nine." His brow furrowed slightly. "Or maybe I am sixty-five."

"I like to play soccer," Mustafa went on eagerly. "What do you like to do, Soraya?"

They worked through the next three chapters before the light started to fade. Then the topic changed, though the language didn't.

"Would you like to cook the food again tonight?" Muhammed asked Soraya.

She didn't care if it ever stopped snowing out there. "Yes."

"Good." He eyed Mustafa. "Then we will go and get more wood."

"How much do we need?" Mustafa didn't wait for an answer. "After Soraya and I live in Australia, Muhammed, and go to school there and work and have money, then we will go to England and see London and say hello to the king and queen." Mustafa chuckled at that and continued to prattle away in English, refusing to speak a word of Farsi, until the wood was in and his first mouthful of kabuli finally silenced him.

Seven

When Muhammed pulled the curtain back the next morning, the window gleamed like a square of butter. He opened the door. Sunlight and snow were everywhere. "The day sparkles," he said in Farsi, bringing in wood and a pot of water. "Allah akbar." This time, he chose to light the fire himself, while his guests started packing up their things.

They ate naan bread and yoghurt quietly before Muhammed spoke again.

"This is the sort of day when mountain travellers concentrate on the sky and snow peaks rather than what's at their feet. You will hear the sound of mines exploding today. Do you have darkened glasses?"

"No," Mustafa answered.

Muhammed searched through a stack of belongings beside his bed and found two pairs of scratched glasses. "Take these. You may return them, Mustafa, when next you come through. Carved on the rock face where we turned off the track yesterday is the letter M. M for Muhammed, M for Mustafa. So you'll always know where to find shelter. Insha'allah." He drew them a detailed map of the track and shaded in where minefields might be, before putting it and a bag of rice into Mustafa's pack. "The track divides further on up. Go right and you go towards Kabul. So stay to the left for the border. Remember that it will be wet and slippery out there. Go slowly and watch out for toy dolls and sections of raised rocks on the track. Mines could lie underneath." At the door, Muhammed turned to Soraya and grinned. "Today I'll scratch out an S next to the M in case you decide to return one day. Manda nabashi."

"Zanda bashi," they chorused, putting on their glasses and leaving him there in the doorway.

Snow on the track was already mushy and stained in grime from earlier travellers. As the sun rose, the track got wetter. Men and pack animals passed going in both directions. Distant shelling started up again then stopped. Amongst the boulders, occasionally, springs could be heard trickling away.

Traversing a slippery section of track hidden away from the sun, they came upon the frozen carcass of a half-eaten horse, its milky eyes the size of small plates, its blood and the mud congealing.

"Hungry?" Mustafa asked, still spouting his English.

As he stepped over it, Soraya scrabbled up rocks and went around.

By midday, Soraya's boots were leaking and her blisters were rubbing hot and sticky again. She asked Mustafa to stop, then sat down on a rock and tightened her laces. It was a sunny, peaceful spot, so she lingered, taking off her glasses and gazing far down into a gorge where a hook-shaped river ran fast and quiet. Her mind wandered to Australia and she pictured herself there. With no burqa, she'd have a face to show people and the freedom to do what she pleased: polish her nails and wear make-up and bright clothes – pants and skirts above her ankles. She'd linger in markets and go to the cinema. And when her hair was long enough again, she'd get it cut in a salon. She'd ride in big, comfortable cars and use electricity, a telephone and running water again. There'd be televisions to turn on and music and dancing and whole days of school and friends, as well as books and magazines to read openly. And surely Ahmed would get to the border, or at least back to Masar e-Sharif safely. And surely her family would follow her to Penrith, in the city of Sydney, where there'd be no Taliban and no rockets and bombs and sky demons falling out of the sky. Where she would be free to work and go outside without a mahram, and meet boys and choose who she would marry, and have babies in hospitals and…

Seeing Mustafa disappear around the next bend brought her mind back. She hopped up and followed him. Beyond the bend, the track narrowed between huge boulders and the steep scree precipice on her left. As she stepped around the first boulder, she heard the high-pitched whinnying of a horse.

Then someone shouted, "You! Stay there!".

Panic-struck, Soraya pressed herself flat against rock and looked around. Nothing moved. There was no one around. Only a bird could have seen her there, she soon realised. So it had to be Mustafa being shouted at. The picture of that frozen horse filled her mind again. Was there another one up ahead about to be eaten? She edged further along, rounding the boulder. The horse's back legs came into view first, then all of it sprawled across the track. A front leg jutted off at a sharp angle. Bone protruded. Blood pooled. Mustafa was a couple of metres away to her right shielding her from the Taliban fighters. Over his shoulder, she saw a fighter walk up to the horse and take aim. BANG! More blood spurted as the gunshot echoed over the gorge.

The fighter replaced his rifle with a long blade knife and started cutting away the bags and boxes from the horse. "You're with others?"

"No, alone," Mustafa answered.

"A pity. But there will be others along soon enough. Drop your pack and take out only what you need for two days. That box will be your pack now."

"Where do I have to take it?" Mustafa asked, setting his pack on the ground.

"Kabul."

"And once I carry it there, will I be free to go?"

"Who can say."

Retreating and quickening her pace. Soraya got back as far as the frozen carcass before scampering up rocks towards a gap between boulders.

"Manda nabashi."

She swung around and spotted Muhammed emerging into sunlight on the track below. A pack was on his back, a walking stick in his hand. "Trouble?" he asked, moving up towards her.

Gawking at him, it took her a moment to answer. "Taliban. They've taken Mustafa and they're coming this way."

"Ah," he sighed, joining her.

They climbed up into the gap and waited.

"Why are you here?" she asked, so pleased he was.

"After you left, I thought how long it's been since I've visited the bazaars of Peshawar, so I…" He stopped and pointed towards the track.

The Taliban moved into view – two at the front and two at the back. Between them were Mustafa and one other porter, half-hidden under their loads.

"Stay here," Muhammed said, surprising her again. He stepped out. "Salaam aleikum."

The fighters stopped and watched him descend.

"Waleikum as'salaam," the leader at the front replied, his rifle in his hands.

"You have a porter with you. His name is Mustafa. I know his family in Masar e-Sharif. Can you tell me if he'll be released soon?"

The fighters glared at him. "Rohani?" the leader asked.

"Balay. The boy's parents are of the faithful. He is their only son."

The fighters exchanged glances. "From Kabul he can go."

"Along a safe route?"

"If he can find one."

"Allah akbar. Can I speak to him?"

"Be quick."

Muhammed went to Mustafa. "You may find Ahmed in Kabul. But whether you do or not, once you're finished, don't linger. Get home. Tell your family what has happened, and that I'm taking Soraya to Peshawar."

"Allah akbar. Tashakor, Muhammed."

Eight

The sun rose over the eastern mountains spilling light down into the valley. Wrapped up in scarves and blankets, Soraya and Zahir – the old village headman – sat together on the only section of boundary wall that hadn't crumbled away and littered the ground. To their right lay the largely abandoned, battle-scarred village. A noisy goat grazed on the roof of the nearest hut. Further away, a rooster crowed. In front of them, through gnarled walnut trees, the headman's wife and Muhammed were stooped over a semi-frozen creek. They chatted, broke up ice with stones and scooped water into a bucket and Muhammed's water bag.

"I think there is more talking than water-collecting going on there," the headman commented, palming his beard that had gone yellow with age. It was the first time he'd initiated any conversation with her in the two days she and Muhammed had been there.

Soraya smiled politely under her scarf. "Muhammed does like to talk." She knew him well enough now to joke about that.

Looking around, it struck her how beautiful mornings could be in these mountains, at least until the day's first fighters, helicopters or planes intruded on the view. Right now, though, there was peace and quiet, and she felt good, better than she had since she'd looked down into that river-filled gorge just before Mustafa was taken. So how long ago was that now? A week? Longer? Long enough, anyway, for the rivers and creeks to slow and turn sluggish again. Being able to sleep indoors here the past two nights felt like a preview of paradise after so many nights spent under rock overhangs in the bone-stabbing cold.

Muhammed's raised voice, followed by the wife's tittering laughter, rang out. In Masar e-Sharif, her legs would have been whipped for laughing like that.

"They talk as if they've known each other forever," Soraya said.

"If not forever, certainly for a very long time."

His sudden willingness to communicate was a pleasant surprise. Though almost everyone in other villages had known Muhammed, no one greeted him with as much warmth and cheerfulness as these two people.

Soraya's curiosity itched and she wondered how long, and under what circumstances, they had known each other. But it was inappropriate to ask such direct questions of a person outside her own family. "I guess being close to a rohani can make people feel that they've known Muhammed for ages."

"Has it with you?"

"Balay." She paused, not knowing how much Muhammed might have told them about her. Yet she wanted to keep the conversation going, and that meant confiding in him. "Without Muhammed, I don't know where I'd be now…lost…maybe dead."

He nodded. "My wife and Muhammed were close before he became a rohani."

"Were they?"

"She is his sister-in-law."

Stunned, it took a moment for Soraya to absorb what that meant. "Then where…?" She stopped.

The goat pawed away at the roof. The rooster still had something to crow about.

The headman eased himself off the wall but, instead of moving away, he just stood there eyeing the ground. "One day," he started, "during the early stages of the war with the Russians, a helicopter came up the valley and hovered over us. It was planting time and no mujahideen freedom fighters were anywhere near here, so we ignored it and just went about our work. Then the helicopter swooped down and fired rockets and bullets at such a furious rate that in minutes ten people lay dead and our village was almost destroyed. As we learned to our great cost that day, war isn't just between those carrying weapons in opposing armies. In this country, war excludes no one." He met her gaze now. "I believe it's a lesson you've learned as well."

"Balay."

Muhammed and the wife lifted their containers and parted, she towards her stone hut, he back up through the trees.

"I will tell you something now for your ears alone," the headman said. "Because you and Muhammed have grown close, you should know that you two have more in common than just this trek you're taking to Peshawar. You see, among the many killed in the helicopter attack that day were Muhammed's wife and three-year-old daughter. His agony was such that he vowed then and there to become a rohani and live solely in the spiritual world with nothing between him and god. Allah akbar. That may be fine for those born to live unknown, which is the rohani's life. But I've never felt he was suited to doing that. I've always viewed him as a man of the soil, of the people, who moved much too easily in the visible world to cut himself off from it. And watching him here with you just verifies that." His voice quickened as Muhammed got close, smiling up at them. "So you should know, Soraya, it's my belief that by accepting his guidance you're benefiting him as much as he's benefiting you… Ah, Muhammed," the headman said to him, smiling. "You've rested well these past two days. You have water and your food is packed. All that remains now is for you and your Peshawar-bound friend here to share a last meal with us."

Muhammed laughed. "As always, Zahir, your kindness is like these mountains – ever present. But before we accept still more of your generous hospitality, tell us about the crops you plan to grow this spring."

As they chatted away, Soraya thought about what Zahir had told her. She recalled a stop they'd made a few days earlier, when Muhammed had descended the few metres to wash in a small stream. After he'd taken off his shirt and quilted coat, she'd glanced at him when she shouldn't have and noticed a bright welt of raised scar tissue below his right collarbone. She thought now that it was probably the right size for a bullet wound.

The rooster was finished for the day, the goat curled up asleep in the sun.

The headman moved off.

"After we eat, we must go," Muhammed noted in more instructional

English, before reverting to Farsi. "We'll be out of these mountains by tomorrow. With good fortune and good weather, we should be in Peshawar in three or four days' time."

Soraya's thoughts were still tied here, though, as she pictured villagers looking up terrified – the din of rockets and gunfire blasting away from above, the sudden explosions and terror and death on the ground. Like the day they saw the American helicopter attacking the village, but much closer, ear-ringing close, being targeted here under some foreigner's gun sight. "I love this village, Muhammed, and these mornings, and being close to people I already feel so much for. If I were a Buddhist, I'd say something about wanting to spend my next lifetime here."

Something on the horizon caught Muhammed's eye. "As you can see, this place hasn't always been so peaceful."

"No, but in time it has become that again," she added quickly, consciously light-hearted. "Allah akbar."

"The secret lies in letting go," he muttered. "Yes. You're right, Soraya. This place, in time, has become peaceful again." He looked around at her, reclaiming his grin. "Well, if in your next lifetime you're to shave your head and don a saffron robe and sandals here, we'd better make it easy for you to find your way back. I saw an old container of paint in the hut I'm in. I'm sure we can find something that'll serve as a brush and paint the letter S on a big boulder here too."

"And an M?"

"For Mustafa, balay."

"And another one for Muhammed?"

His grin widened. "If that's what you want."

"Do you think there'll be enough paint for an A as well?"

"For Ahmed. We'll make sure there is. But any more and I don't think we'll be getting out of here today."

"Then K for Karima, R for Rahman, N for…"

*

48

When they dropped down into softer hills, scattered with freshly painted villages, wheat fields and working irrigation channels, Muhammed told her a story. It was about Zahir, his wife and their son, Saeed, who was studying in Peshawar now. When Saeed finished his education and started working, he was going to lease a small shop-house for his parents, further east in Rawalpindi or Lahore, and move them there. Muhammed talked about how proud Zahir and his wife were of Saeed and he mentioned that he hoped to visit the boy in Peshawar.

With his eyes fastened on the track, Muhammed continued the story. He told her about the day a Russian helicopter came over the valley. As mujahideen fighters never stopped in Zahir's village, people took little notice of it hovering over them. But they should have. For the helicopter attacked and killed many people, including the two daughters of Zahir and his wife.

"The secret lies in letting go," Soraya mimicked.

He heard. "For those who have known such horror, there can be no greater struggle in life than to gain the inner strength to do that…I would think."

Other tracks merged with theirs. The number of people increased. Haggard figures, carrying bundled belongings strapped to their backs, moved along in their direction. Young fighters from Pakistan trooped past heading the other way. Some carried guns and grenade launchers, others nothing. In surrounding fields, colourfully dressed villagers with big noses and small brown eyes stared at them. They often called out to one another and said things Soraya couldn't understand. Her mind skipped back to Zahir's village and stayed there until they stopped under poplar trees to camp for the night.

Nine

Now it was their turn to stare. Masar e-Sharif and the many villages she and Muhammed had passed through were cities of gold compared to this.

While new arrivals streamed down the hill, they sat on their heels and, through a vast brown smear of smoke and dust, scanned the sea of humanity and dun-coloured tents that blended in with the earth down there. North and south, the encampment stretched beyond their vision, though the eastern edge was clearly visible. It ended in line with three massive tents emblazoned with large red crosses on their roofs like target markers for space demons. Further on, across the barren ground, guard stands and barbed wire fencing marked the Pakistani border.

Having got this far, the goal of every Afghani narrowed to the pitted access road that crossed into Pakistan like a pathway to heaven. The area between the encampment and that road teemed with armed men and swaying trucks and buses hurling up great plumes of road dust in their eagerness to get to their destination, unload passengers and return to Kabul for more.

"I ask myself," Soraya said, trying to comprehend all that was going on below them, "could Ahmed be down there? And if he is, how would I ever find him?"

"If he is, he would know which direction we'd be coming from."

She got to her feet. "Will you stay close?"

"Only your pack will be closer."

Entering the encampment, the smell of raw sewage strengthened. Men and boys squatted around small fires tending cooking pots. Smoke drifted. People coughed. Big-eyed babies cried. Kneeling figures on filthy robes prayed. Women scurried in and out of the patchwork tents. Girls her age carried children on their hips – rocking them and wiping their noses. Soraya looked back regularly to check that her mahram was still behind her, before stopping and describing Ahmed and Mustafa to people and asking if they'd seen them. Most shook their heads in a daze. One raised his upturned hands to the sky, as if about to pray, then looked at her like she was a lunatic. Undeterred, she kept trying, until four gunshots rang out behind them.

"A boy is born," bellowed a man sitting in the dirt below her. "Allah akbar."

"Allah akbar," others chorused flatly, before staring at the ground.

"In Kabul, I met Ahmed."

So close and unexpected was the accented voice that Soraya thought she imagined it. She turned around. Between a pakhool cap and a partially scarf-wrapped face, a pair of black, slanted eyes glared at her. She recognised them as belonging to a Hazara, the Taliban's decreed enemy.

"Ahmed? You met Ahmed?" she checked, incredulous.

He nodded. From his pocket, he took out several scrappy bits of paper with writing on them. He fingered through them until he found the one he was after. His eyes locked on hers again. "You are his sister, Soraya?"

She felt like pinching herself to ensure she was really there. "Balay."

He moved closer, lowering his scarf to reveal his youthful, flat-faced features. He glanced over at Muhammed. "Manda nabashi."

"Zanda bashi."

"I am Amir Yaqub. Like your brother, Ahmed, I too have been a captive of the Taliban in Kabul. To keep our spirits up there, we captives talked together – when we could – about escaping, particularly to Pakistan. We decided to write messages to relatives who might be at the border or, insha'allah, across it in Peshawar. We included descriptions and exchanged copies of the messages." He patted the lump of paper in his pocket. "And we made a vow that if any of us escaped and, by god's guidance, met up with someone's relative, we'd make ourselves known and hand over their message. Three days ago, as the Taliban were retreating from the capital, I alone managed to escape." He handed over the folded piece of paper. "Anyway, I believe this is for you."

She thanked him, still stunned. "My cousin Mustafa was also taken to Kabul by the Taliban."

"There are so many who were. I'm sorry, I did not meet him."

Amir and Muhammed edged away as she opened her note.

Mustafa and Soraya –
     Allah akbar. He has heard my prayers and worked yet another miracle! For this note has reached you. It is enough for you to know I'm alive and waiting for an opportunity to escape also. Insha'allah. Do you know the Northern Alliance has retaken Masar e-Sharif, and it won't be long before Kabul falls too. But this will not stop the fighting, so YOU TWO MUST NOT STOP OR THINK OF RETURNING until you have been delivered to Pervez Lateef in Peshawar. To give hope to what remains of our family, you must journey on to that beautiful peaceful land of Australia and make a new start for us. I cannot write any smaller, or pray any harder for that to happen. GET THERE, PLEASE.
     Ahmed

As she looked up, shots rang out again – not the two for the birth of a girl, the four for a boy, but a barrage of gunfire that turned everyone's heads towards the middle of the encampment. When it stopped, shouting could be heard, interspersed with more gunfire that spread and moved their way.

"Jihad! Jihad!"

Tat – tat – tat –tat – tat – tat.

"Defend Afghanistan from the great Satan!"

Tat – tat – tat – tat.

"Jihad! Jihad!"

Tat – tat – tat – tat – tat – tat.

"Death to the infidel! Death to America, the enemy of humanity!"

Spaces opened up as people slipped back into their tents. Amir must have as well, for he suddenly disappeared.

Tat – tat – tat – tat – tat – tat.

More chanting broke out. Those who remained outside stood and joined in, beating the air with their fists. "Jihad! Jihad! Jihad!"

"Don't run," Muhammed warned her. "Just keep your eyes on that hill in front of us and with a steady pace lead us back up it."

Descending refugees were of two minds now. Some sat along the track's edge visibly measuring their options. Others realised they didn't have any and, despite the growing wave of chaos and danger, stepped warily down the track, fingering worry beads and mouthing prayers.

At the top of the hill, a voice called out, "Soraya!"

They turned and saw Amir running towards them, using his scarf to dab a bleeding nose. "In my eagerness to get away," he explained, drawing level with them, "I neglected to ask a family if they minded me sharing their tent."

"They weren't Hazara, then?" Muhammed asked.

A wry grin showed on Amir's face. "I was in too much of a hurry to ask but, no, it would seem they weren't. And neither are you," he continued, "so, not wishing to repeat the same mistake, I won't impose myself on you…unless…"

"We're not traveling with a tent," Soraya commented.

"I'm not at all anxious to get back into one."

"You're welcome to travel with us," Soraya said. He was polite and spoke like an educated person. More importantly, he knew Ahmed and had nowhere else to go. She stepped closer. "We know of a border crossing north of here where there are no guards or refugee camps."

"Should we meet up with Taliban, you do know the dangers of travelling with an Hazara?" His eyes lingered on Muhammed for a moment. "Even being a rohani won't help with many of them."

Muhammed stayed quiet, which didn't surprise Soraya. That was another thing she considered special about him now, the way he was encouraging her to make more and more decisions. "Then we'll have to be careful not to run into any, won't we, Muhammed?"

"Insha'allah."

Ten

A huge yellow cloud enveloped her, but did nothing to deaden the sound storm that raged on all around her. *Jihad! Jihad! Jihad!* Helicopter blades beat overhead, jet engines shrieked and sky demons howled across the sky. Tat – tat – tat – tat – tat –tat…Whoosh. Bullets and rockets zipped past. Explosions shook mountains, echoed down valleys and loosened great boulders that thundered down burying people, tents and villages below. *Death to the infidel! Death to the great Satan!*

"Satan is close," she tried to tell those voices. "Hell is here." But they wouldn't hear of it.

Death to America, the enemy of humanity!

The yellow cloud thickened. It got hotter and began to swirl with blood and shredded arms and legs.

Her mother called out, "I love you, Soraya."

"Where are you, Mama? Come and hold me, please, Mama." But it was as though she'd suddenly lost her voice for, no matter how hard she tried to scream, nothing came out but a whisper.

A thickly bearded man in a black turban stepped out of the cloud and leered down at her, a cable whip in his hand. His eyes pulsated red. Blood seeped out of his nose and dripped to the ground. "Your burqa," he said with a slow grin. He ran his tongue over stained, broken teeth. "Where is it?" His eyes swelled. He lifted his whip high up into the hot, swirling cloud.

"No! Please! Please!"

"Sshh, Soraya. It's all right. It's all right."

Someone finally heard her.

"Sshh."

Muhammed. No, not you! My auntie's got my burqa, not you, NOT YOU!

She woke to hard sunlight, her heart a fist banging away in her chest. Truck horns blared. People shouted. An engine vibrated beneath her, sending tremours through her as if she were suffering from malaria. Their trishaw was stalled in a traffic jam. Wrapped in a blanket, their driver shook his fist and shouted out at a horse cart broken down in front of them.

She lifted her head off Amir's shoulder. "Sorry."

"Don't be. Had you woken up a few minutes earlier, it would have been me apologising to you."

"Welcome back to Peshawar," Muhammed said, on her right.

It all flashed back to her now — the night spent climbing over rocks getting across the border, then trying to sleep cold and scared under another rock overhang. The low morning sun lighting up the hills and wheat fields and villages below. And this driver — a yawning resident of one of them — recognising a rohani and offering to bring them into the city as a gift to start the day.

As the flow of traffic set off again, their driver leaned back and shouted to Muhammed in English, "Khyber Bazaar come soon!"

They stared out at the footpath stalls, broken neon signs and row upon row of multistoreyed shops packed with merchandise, before their driver shouted out again, "Now Khyber Bazaar!"

He swept the steering wheel around and leaned into a turn that sent them veering across the path of a truck. Brakes shrieked. The truck's horn blasted their ears from so close it seemed to be mounted on their seat. Their trishaw sped up. More horns blared and drivers screamed, hoisting their fists into the air and shaking their heads in disbelief.

"Are you okay?" Muhammed asked her.

"Balay." She took a deep, bolstering breath. "And you?"

"At my age, being flattened by a truck wouldn't count for much."

Close to their destination now, they'd soon be going their separate ways. "It would to me." Her throat tightened. Muhammed was her guide and saviour. Without him, what? Wishful thoughts filled her mind. Maybe they wouldn't find Pervez Lateef. Maybe he'd left the city, or died.

Or if he was here, maybe he'd gone out of business. Or if he hadn't, maybe he had too many people to send to Australia and he'd say to her, "I'm sorry, Soraya. I can't help you now. You can take your father's money if you'd like or you can return in six months, or a year. Insha'allah." And she'd quietly rejoice. Her father's voice sounded in her head. *So you must demonstrate how right she could be, Soraya.* Ahmed's note crowded in. *GET THERE, PLEASE.* Well, if they couldn't find this Pervez Lateef, or if he couldn't help her, what was she supposed to do, swim to Australia?

"We're here." Muhammed said, as they stopped next to the crowded footpath.

Once out of the trishaw, Amir offered some coins to the driver.

"No, no. My day is blessed having a rohani as a first passenger."

"Take it from the girl and me then," Amir persisted.

"Allah akbar." The driver grabbed the coins, then launched his three-wheeled vehicle back into the traffic.

Moving into the bazaar, Amir dropped more coins to entryway beggars – amputees on protheses and old men with walking sticks. Inside, he and Soraya marvelled at how huge and crowded the place was. Three levels, each seemingly without a beginning or end. A central courtyard and an open gallery were on the ground floor. Everywhere else was a maze of dark passageways full of overstuffed shops and shoppers, hawkers and money changers, foot-powered sewing machines, racked rugs and boys in shorts beating them with sticks. Pakistani pop music blared. Vendors and customers shouted. An elevated television set played for lingering onlookers. No black-turbaned police here to whip them on. No blood-encrusted hands, feet or nail-polished fingers dangling down for them to avoid. Just music and screen entertainment and, yes, a few burqas, but mostly men in skullcaps and full-faced women free to choose what they wore and to move when they wanted to. It was mayhem, but it felt so free and deliciously good.

Amir was as disoriented as Soraya, but Muhammed remained unfazed and took the lead. It wasn't until they visited their fourth rug shop that someone took the time to notice that Muhammed was a rohani, so admitted they knew the location of Pervez Lateef's rug shop.

"Third level, at the back," the merchant said, "but before you buy anything there, please remember I will sell it to you at a cheaper price."

Soraya's eyes found her feet. He was here. He hadn't gone out of business, or died. So that left just one tiny possibility.

It took them half an hour to find the shop, which turned out to be bigger than the others. It was brightly lit and had beautiful hand-knotted rugs hanging from long racks on the walls. In the corner, sitting behind a polished desk, was a boy in a long white Pakistani shirt and loose trousers. He sprang off his stool and welcomed them before they'd even got through the door. After Muhammed introduced everyone and asked for Pervez Lateef, the boy deflated a little and retreated through a curtained doorway into the backroom. A moment later, he returned, grabbing a serving tray and motioning for them to go in.

Two heavy men, with neatly trimmed beards and dressed in perfectly laundered cotton pants, white over-shirts and skull caps, stood together facing them.

The older man on the right spoke first to Muhammed, as was the custom. "I'm Pervez Lateef and this is my brother, Wajed."

Their meaty, ring-adorned hands were extended to both Muhammed and Amir. Pervez Lateef looked puzzled when Amir introduced himself, but quickly invited them to sit down on cushions that lined the walls. The boy entered with sizzling kebabs, a pot of tea and cups, and proceeded to serve everyone.

After he left, Pervez Lateef eyed Amir again. "You are not Ahmed Zadran?"

"No."

For the first time, Lateef looked over at Soraya. "But you are Soraya Zadran."

She found it difficult to return his gaze. "Balay. My brother Ahmed was taken by the Taliban, as was my cousin Mustafa. Muhammed and Amir have helped me get to Peshawar."

Lateef thanked both men as though he was Soraya's guardian now. "Please," he went on, "these fine kebabs are made for eating hot."

Ten minutes later, rohani acknowledged and food eaten, Lateef spoke to Soraya. "I will try to let your father know what has happened. But it won't be easy. Your country is in turmoil and my contacts there are difficult to maintain. However, you'll be pleased to know that everything has been arranged for you. Your journey to Australia will begin in four or five days…"

And with that Soraya's spirits tumbled.

"In the meantime, as part of the agreement with your father, there is a room for you to stay in not far from here. A café just down the road will provide your meals until you get your travel documents and are driven to Islamabad to board your plane."

"And that plane will take her straight to Australia?" Muhammed asked.

Lateef found it odd that a rohani could be interested in such things. But then the answer was no great secret, if it were phrased in the right terms. "From Islamabad, she will fly to Indonesia."

"And from there where will she go?"

Lateef poured himself more tea and sampled it noisily before examining his nails. "From there she will sail to the northern city of Darwin on a passenger ship. The leisurely trip will take four days. When the ship docks, the first thing she'll notice is how hospitable Australian people are. They will wave and shout their greetings and helpful officials will be there to assist her with accommodation, food and clothing, schooling and…" – he paused to glance over and smile at her – "and of course everyone there has a television set."

"Paradise," Muhammed muttered, without enthusiasm, over his cup.

"Indeed," Lateef answered over his.

"Your business must be thriving."

"Indeed," Lateef repeated. "Such has been the popularity of our migration program that it has out-performed all our other businesses – rugs, transport, pharmaceuticals." He turned his attention to Amir. "And may I ask what your plans are here in Peshawar?"

"To find work."

"That's not easy for…for any Afghani."

Amir preferred words to allusions. "Not easy for any Afghani who happens to be Hazara?"

Lateef shrugged his shoulders, avoiding a direct response. "Once Soraya is settled in today, perhaps you'd like to return. If you do, I might be able to offer you what you're looking for."

Amir showed his surprise and renewed his respectful tone. "Tashakor, I will."

"And Muhammed, do you plan to stay long in Peshawar?"

He glanced at Soraya before answering, "Four or five days."

Lateef smiled his understanding and extended his hands palms up towards him. "For a rohani, for that amount of time, there is a small room available on the floor above Soraya's. Just big enough for two of you, I would think. While I cannot offer you food, I can offer you this room without cost."

"You are kind," Muhammed said, his face a blank.

Lateef nodded in apparent agreement, looking pleased that he had his hold on everyone now.

The boy was summoned. Issued with instructions, he led them out of the bazaar and down a crowded alleyway with tangled power lines like spider webs slung across the thin slot of sky over them. No vapour trails for eyes to follow here. Wrapped up in back-street noise, there'd be no sounds of sky demons, jets or beating helicopter blades either, just the soothing prattle of motor scooters and the sounds of voices and laughter and children playing. A pity she couldn't stay here for the next fifty years, she thought as Lateef's voice switched on in her head. *They will wave and shout their greetings and helpful officials will be there to assist...* Would all that really happen? Hopefully, for it now seemed that nothing would prevent her from finding out. She diverted her mind by concentrating on what was around her in the alley.

In the absence of sunlight, gaslight bathed the small shop-houses. Boys played a flat bat and ball game she'd not seen before. Grease-streaked men stooped over motor scooters and bikes and battered vehicles. Everyone seemed to be doing something and no one carried any weapons or whips.

Through an open doorway and up rickety stairs to the third floor they went, then down a creaking hallway, past rooms, random voices and a toilet door before coming to Soraya's room. The door squeaked as it was opened and they were shown in. An open window above the alleyway racket was at the opposite end. A small wooden table with a candle, and a bed with a thin mattress were on one side. A couple of cushions were tossed against the wall on the other. What those power lines out there were used for, other than hanging washing on, she had no idea. But it didn't matter. Her room felt luxurious.

*

Soraya napped and woke up to her English book before Muhammed and Amir came in.

They sat down on the cushions and, noticing her book, Muhammed told her in a mixture of Farsi and English that he'd sold some gemstones at the bazaar and managed to locate where Saeed lived. It wasn't far. He'd talked to him briefly and Saeed was anxious to meet her. They could visit him any evening that was convenient. He went quiet for a moment looking over at Amir, who seemed preoccupied. "Ask him where he's been," Muhammed said to her.

"Accepting Pervez Lateef's invitation to visit him again," Amir replied.

"Could he help you?"

"In a way that was completely unexpected." He looked around the room before eyeing Soraya again. "I should explain something to you." He paused, seemingly reluctant to go on. "When I used to live with my family in a village outside Bamiyan, I sometimes got work as a truck driver. I had a truck in the village the day the Taliban attacked us two years ago. My father and older brother were killed, along with many others. But before that happened, I was given what money we had and told to drive my mother, sister and other women to safety. An hour's drive from the village is a large cave. We'd almost got there when the truck broke down. There were no tools, so we walked to the cave, unnoticed, and hid there.

Eventually I got my mother and sister to Herat, where I bought the last two places on a bus going to the Iranian border. I told them I would come the next day and meet them there. But the next morning I was told their bus had struck a landmine on a mountain road and rolled over the edge." His eyes grew thinner as he fastened them on the window. "No one survived. A few days later, the Taliban took me off a bus I was travelling on to Masar e-Sharif. They beat me, but apparently got little satisfaction from doing so, as there was nothing in me that still felt any pain. So rather than kill me, they made me a porter and I carried their supplies to Kabul. The rest you know, okay?"

She sat on the edge of the bed, stunned and mystified. "Okay."

"I was a mahram then, you understand that?"

"Balay."

"And we were only going to be apart for one single day and that happened."

"I'm sorry, Amir."

"But, the thing is, Soraya, Lateef has suggested that I become a mahram again."

"Whose?"

"Yours."

"But...how? We aren't in the same family. Besides, Muhammed is staying in Peshawar until I go."

"Not here, but in places where it won't make any difference that we're not related."

Pieces began to fall into place. "Indonesia and Australia, you mean?"

"That was his suggestion."

Shock turned to acceptance, then to pleasure. Her smile showed it. She eyed Muhammed for his reaction. "He's coming with me, he says."

Pleasure was there for him too. He grinned. "Apparently."

"Isn't that good?"

But Amir remained silent and still appeared troubled.

And that's what made her think a piece or two was still missing. She recalled the story he'd just told. *I'd been given what money we had and...*

Her mood cooled. So who was paying? Amir? How could he? Lateef ? Why would he? Or was it her father, now that Ahmed wasn't going? It wasn't a question she'd have asked him in Afghanistan. Even here, where open-faced women in colourful chadors lingered and laughed, it was probably inappropriate. But she felt she had a right to know. "Do you have the money to go?"

"I will have in four days' time."

Relief was instant, but so was remorse. She scolded herself for being so mean-spirited. "After robbing a bank, you mean?" Here, as opposed to Afghanistan, they were still open for business, she'd noticed.

Her joking steered him away from the past. His face brightened. "After driving one of Lateef's trucks up to the north-west frontier to pick up cargo and bring it back."

"The equivalent of a year's wages for less than a week's work," Muhammed chipped in, his brow furrowing slightly. "Did he mention what the cargo was?"

"No. But then I didn't ask. Just one trip up there and back, followed by a much longer trip to Australia, where I'll know no one, but where we'll be greeted by happy, helpful people who will give us an opportunity to rebuild our lives, raise families and become citizens of a great country." He eyed Soraya again. "So that's why I told you that story. For you to know that I must try to be a better mahram for you in Indonesia and Australia than I have been in Afghanistan."

"I couldn't want for a better one, Amir."

Sharing a table together at the nearby café that night, they ate well and told bright stories that mirrored their moods. Well, at least she and Amir did, while Muhammed seemed content to just sit and listen. Their minds shot forward and they talked about Australia and what they would do there.

Soraya put into words what had previously stayed in her thoughts. She would study hard and attend university. She'd become a teacher, like her auntie. "Imagine the look on her face when she finds out about that," she said. Her classroom would be lined with books and have big windows and distant views. And she'd choose to marry someone as warm and compassionate as the two she was free to sit with here. And she'd have babies – two, maybe three…well, at least as many as it took to have a girl, anyway, because they were equal to boys over there, weren't they? And she just wanted to do things with her daughter that her mother did with her, except perhaps sew. And this is how she described her house to them: there'd be running water, electricity and a garden to grow things and friendly neighbours and room enough for her children to play without ever having to use a street. By then, hopefully, her family would be there. And together, they'd drive in a car to places and have picnics and watch the boys play soccer, and maybe even the girls too, though she didn't know if she could ever get used to that happening.

Watching Muhammed, as he watched her, slowed her down. Of course, if she worked very hard, she said to them, maybe one day she'd have the money to come back and visit people who were very special to her.

After the call to prayer the next morning, Lateef's boy came and took Amir away. While he was gone, she and Muhammed visited the hospitable Saeed twice, and worshipped in mosques and wandered the city.

On the afternoon of their fifth day there, Lateef's boy returned with a message. Lateef wanted to see her as soon as possible. She decided not to contact Muhammed, but to demonstrate her independence by going to see Lateef on her own. There on his back-room cushions, while he drank tea and ate kebabs, Lateef announced that she would be leaving for Islamabad in the morning.

"But Amir hasn't returned," she said.

Pausing to sip his tea, he nodded his understanding, then leaned forward and surprised her by patting her knee. "There's been a slight change of plans," he noted, with a smile that did nothing to ease her discomfort.

Her father's warning rang out in her head. *Never trust fat men in poor places.*

"Amir will meet you at Islamabad Airport." Lateef handed over her travel documents then explained what passports and visas were for, and how to present them and her plane tickets, and what would happen when she arrived in Jakarta.

She thanked him, then asked boldly, "Does Amir have everything he needs?"

"Of course," Lateef replied, before apologising for his inability to accompanying her to Islamabad. He then suggested how she could protect herself from the sun while cruising to Australia. He told her about animals called kangaroos and koalas that were everywhere there. When she had trouble pronouncing those words, he passed her a slip of paper and a biro. Patting her knee again, he spelled the words in English so she could write them down. After she had, she stood up, thanked him again and left.

That evening at the café, the discomfort of her knee being touched by a stranger was gradually replaced by a buzzing excitement about what lay ahead. In answer to Muhammed's questions, she showed him her documents, and explained in detail what they were for and what was going to happen. He listened, nodded and ate little.

The next morning a mini-bus rumbled down the alleyway. Muhammed obviously heard it, for he was at her door seconds after it stopped. As they descended the stairs, she wanted to tell him things, but her tears made that difficult too.

The mini-bus was like all the others in the city, except the windows were blacked out and no one was sitting on the roof or hanging on the railings outside. The driver checked her name then became impatient for her to get in.

"Wish Amir well for me," Muhammed said.

"I will." The effort to control her tears was lost. All she could do was dab away at them. "I wouldn't have got here, I wouldn't be doing any of this if you hadn't helped me." He must sleep grinning, she thought, before he began to blur again.

"Everything you're feeling I'm feeling as well."

She wouldn't need to wash her face any time soon. It was getting a good enough soaking right now. "Don't let the paint wear off those boulders."

"No."

The driver gunned the engine.

She'd probably lose her lips for doing this in Afghanistan, she thought, as she leaned close, stood up on tiptoes and kissed him on his hairy face. "Thank you, Muhammed."

"Towards God is the journeying, Soraya."

*

There was barely enough light to study her English on the back seat. Besides that, the bus swerved, shuddered to stops and lurched forward so much, it was impossible to keep her eyes on the words, a fact that was further complicated by the raw state of her emotions and a rohani who filled her mind now like family. Leaving Peshawar was like leaving Masar e-Sharif earlier. Though, perhaps, the future was a little bit clearer, Australia a little bit closer. And yes, she was alone this time, but only as far as Islamabad. And this time there'd be no Taliban lurking around the next bend to abduct her mahram. She stashed her book and focused on the other passengers. She counted sixteen in all, excluding her. Only the Pakistani man across from her was not an Afghani.

Specks of black paint had chipped away from the window, so she squinted out occasionally and watched bits of Peshawar then the villages flash by. The faint mist that rose off the fields reminded her of another village – crumbled, almost empty and certainly smaller than these.

While she watched the valley slide into shadow out there, recent voices grew active in her mind, including her own. *Don't let the paint wear off those boulders.*

The bus climbed, rounded sharp bends and finally dropped down into the huge city of Islamabad. Flame trees and bright hibiscus flowers lined the wide, clean streets. In the many small parks, adults sat on benches and children played, and roses and jasmine bloomed. How her mother would have loved this place, she thought, as the mini-bus slowed and became immersed in thick traffic.

She forced herself to think about the future and Australia. People worshipped Christianity there, didn't they? So women didn't wear chadors over their heads. What else did Pervez Lateef say? Ah yes, the tropical seas and the need to protect yourself from the sun. Thinking about Lateef reminded her of the names of those two animals she'd written down. She got out the slip of paper, studied the names and practised saying them three times each. "Kan-ga-roo… Ko-a-la…"

Soft clapping sounded opposite her. She glanced over at the Pakistani man. "Very-good," he said to her.

Language therapy, Muhammed had called it. Embarrassed, Soraya started to apologise, when another sound whined and screamed in overhead. "No!" she cried out, falling to the floor. She waited, terrified and trembling. But no explosion came and the noise died away to nothing. She lifted her eyes.

The man's legs and feet were side-on in the aisle. The rest of him was side-on too, waiting for her to make eye contact. "Aero-plane," he said, leaning forward out of concern. "Only an aero-plane." His smile was there to comfort her. "In Indonesia, pesawat terbang. Like the aeroplane to Indonesia for you and me and ev-er-y-body."

"Yes. Thank you. I am sorry," she replied in their shared language. She realised then that he wasn't practising. He was only going slowly for her sake.

Gawking passengers grabbed their wide-eyed children and turned back round.

Minutes later, the man said, as though to a child, "We are at the air-port now."

When they stopped and got out, two men in dark glasses were there to guide them through the chaos of people and traffic into the terminal. Not seeing Amir there, she presumed he was at the place where they showed their tickets, or maybe on the plane, wherever that was. Yes – that plane. Fear clawed away at her. This is Pakistan, she reminded herself. Where women without burqas stopped to linger and laugh, and where they ate meals with men and boarded planes on their own. It made little difference where she was, though. The thought of that plane's vapour trail continued to send cold tremours through her, even as they were all bundled into a small room where their minders counted heads and collected their documents.

After the number count was finished, a minder called out, "That's everyone, then."

"No, it isn't," Soraya quickly corrected him. "There's one more. His name's Amir Yaqub." She described him.

The minders traded glances. "No. Perhaps tomorrow he will come."

"No. That's not right. In exchange for driving Mister Lateef's truck, it was arranged that he would be here today. He's my mahram." Panic rose. Her voice went with it. "Today! Mister Lateef organised it for today! So he must be here, somewhere. We'll have to find him!"

"I think he will come tomorrow, or the next day."

"I can't go without him! I need to speak to somebody else about this!" Her desperate eyes locked on the open doorway. "There are telephones out there in the terminal. Please help me to telephone Mister Lateef so he can…"

A sealed note was thrust in her face. "From Mister Lateef. It will explain everything. I'll give it to you as soon as you get on the plane."

Eleven

Dear Soraya

Amir is dead.

I'm sorry. With everything that's happening to you now, I thought it better that you didn't hear about this until later on, if then. The fact that you're reading this means that wasn't possible.

I don't know exactly what happened, other than Amir was shot. Banditry, certainly, but who the bandits were and why they attacked my truck, I don't know.

When you are settled in Australia, write to me, care of the Khyber Bazaar, Peshawar. I should then know enough about his death to provide you with details.

I trust your journey will be a pleasant one.

Yours truly,

Pervez Lateef

Soraya rolled the note into a ball and looked around. When she was younger, she'd made drawings of aeroplanes. They had swept-back wings and guns, and their bombs exploded on people and buildings in great red fire stars that could fill up half her drawing paper. Inside a plane for the first time and beyond fear now, Soraya realised all the mistakes she'd made. She'd only drawn the outsides, so it didn't matter about the fields of seats inside aeroplanes. But she had no idea just how huge planes could be, and she'd only ever drawn a single window at the front of them. The fact that they had lines of windows, like transparent scales, running down the great length of their metal skins never entered her head. And on this plane, she sat next to one.

Had Amir been sitting beside her, or Muhammed or Mustafa or Ahmed, rather than an older Pakistani couple, she'd probably have gone all stiff and hot with fear. She didn't. And that puzzled her at first as the plane moved, roared and shot off down that smooth, empty road like a sky demon before rising steeply with such force, she thought she'd stay pinned to her seat all the way to Indonesia. But that thought didn't bother her either, nor did the one about the plane falling out of the sky and hitting the earth in an explosion of body parts, fire and smoke. Because she just didn't care. Feelings had been left behind, and her body left a shell again. How did Amir put it about the Taliban beating him? *There was nothing in me that still felt any pain.* That's what it was like for her too after her mother's death, before she met Muhammed. And that's what it was like again now. But this time, Soraya told herself, it would stay that way forever.

When the plane flattened out and pressure on her ears and body eased, she assumed they were riding the vapour trail, but she couldn't see it down there below them. There was only the dun-coloured earth speckled with patches of green, before darker hills showed and merged into snow-topped mountains.

She sat there strapped in, waiting for another big airport, Indonesia, a ship, Australians waving and shouting their greetings and her uncle in a place called Penrith. She stared at a soundless television fastened to the roof, and at other passengers with wires attached to their ears staring as well – up at the television. It reminded her of the bazaar in Peshawar, although sound blared out there. Perhaps that's what the wires were for, she concluded. She got out her English book and tried to study, but didn't get very far.

The snow peaks grew and reached up through clouds to an immense sky of hard, lonely blue.

"Himalayas," said the Pakistani woman next to her, hovering at her shoulder.

Soraya had read about these mountains in storybooks.

"Mmm," the husband uttered.

Food and drink came: rice, kebabs, melon and tea. Like that served in the backroom of Lateef's shop. Indifferent as she felt, she'd not eaten since the previous night. She did so now, hungrily.

The earth turned a brown smudge down there.

"The plains of India, may they turn to dust in the heat and blow away in the wind."

"Mmm."

She'd heard about the hatred between the Pakistanis and Indians – as strong as that between the Taliban and Hazaras. She glanced down at Lateef's balled-up note between her feet. Were the Taliban in Pakistan also? Were they the bandits? Or did Amir go back into Afghanistan? Wherever he got shot, it was Lateef who sent him there, then instructed his minders not to tell her, or lie to her if that didn't work. So if he could hide the truth about that, what else was he capable of hiding?

She passed the time staring. They must have climbed higher. Below them was their spreading vapour trail, blanketing the earth, absorbing its colour.

She worked out where a toilet was. Excusing herself, she escaped her strapped seat and the Pakistanis, walked up the aisle and turned looking for a doorknob that wasn't there. She waited for someone else to come. A man soon did. He slid a latch on the door and, once inside, slid it back again. And she'd almost gone in there. Her shell weakened as certain feelings slipped back – embarrassment, confusion. At least now she knew how to get in these toilets, but working out which ones were for women was going to take more time.

The man came out.

Soraya waited. A woman came moments later and stunned her by going into the same toilet the man used. She stood there bewildered. If only she knew how long it was going to take for this aeroplane to get back on the ground and let her out.

An attendant approached smiling, and asked if she spoke English.

"A little bit," Soraya answered, bowing her head and folding her arms tightly.

"Do-you-need-any-help?"

More feelings returned: discomfort, frustration. Determination followed. If she couldn't solve this problem on her own, what hope would she have with bigger problems that were sure to confront her in new, very strange countries? "Please, how much time to get to Indonesia?"

The attendant looked at her watch. "About four and a half hours."

Soraya had no choice but to ask her the other question.

"On this plane, the toilets are for both men and women," the attendant answered, reaching over and opening the door of the nearest one. "This one is empty."

The brilliant light knocked Soraya backwards. Fortunately, no one was close enough to notice, or hear the instructions she got on the use of the door and what all the shiny buttons, levers and handles inside were for. The only thing the lady neglected to warn her about was the terrifying noise – like the bottom falling out of the aeroplane – when she pushed the lever and everything dropped out of the toilet into their vapour trail below.

She let her nerves settle, but didn't leave immediately once they had. She just sat there and let a strange wave of comfort wash over her. Ironically, that's what she felt now in this tiny space, cut off from the strange world on the other side of that door. If she'd known how to turn that skin-heating light off, and enclose herself further, she would have. It was certainly warm and bright enough without it.

Minutes passed. Door levers slid back and forth out there. She heard voices and told herself she'd have to leave soon. The attendant was probably staring at her watch and wondering if she'd survived the experience. As she was probably facing in the general direction of Mecca, perhaps she could loudly chant her prayers to gain additional time. Then her eyes brimmed with tears, her throat burned. She dropped her head and cried.

Scolding herself minutes later, Soraya vowed to compensate for another tearful lapse by praying for Amir every day, as she did for her own family and Muhammed. And as soon as she got settled in Australia, she'd write that letter to Pervez Lateef asking... No, women were strong in Australia, weren't they? She'd demand to know every last detail of Amir's death, because...well, because from now on she was going to be tough and strong and indifferent to pain, wasn't she? She was going to withdraw into the inner core of herself and keep an iron grip on her emotions. Though, without her burqa, that would be harder to do in Australia. Well, it was best she didn't have her burqa with her then, wasn't it? It would force her to deal with everything up-front, with no screened barriers or easy hiding places. That being so, she asked herself, what was she doing hiding away in here?

Soraya got up and washed her hands in a surge of water that splattered everywhere. Shaking her hands dry, she looked up and suddenly saw more of herself than she ever had before. The word 'detail' came to mind, for the power of that light and the clarity of that huge mirror worked like an artist's finest brush in drawing it out of her. She wore her mother's favourite chador, its gemstone green the colour of their large eyes. She lifted the chador off her head, placed it loosely around her neck and watched it flow off her shoulders. She leaned closer and studied her open face. Her hair had grown since she'd last seen herself in Masar e-Sharif. It was lustrous in this light and almost covered her ears now, but needed about another year's growth to match her mother's length, her own length before she'd left home. Like her hair, her surprisingly clear skin didn't appear as dark in this light.

She used her fingers like a blind person to appraise herself. She brushed them over that new skin, through her hair, down the pencil-straight ridgeline of her nose and along that ugly worm of scar tissue on her upper lip. Lipstick would cover that, she thought, though she'd have to watch someone else put it on first before she tried to. She sight-measured her long eyelashes next, then finger-traced an eyebrow, a high cheekbone and her jaw that merged with the soft V of her chin. Her eyes, lashes and eyebrows pleased her, but it was her mountain-aired skin that impressed her the most.

A knock came. "Everything-all-right-in-there?"

"Balay – uh, yes. I come out now." She raised her chin defiantly and told herself it was time to face the world as a tough person.

Back out there, though, it didn't take long for her chin to droop and for this nightmare to catch up with her again. How she used to fume about having to wear her burqa everywhere and be escorted by a mahram. Now she felt disoriented and vulnerable without them. How can you keep a vow, she asked herself in frustration, if that vow contradicts what you truly feel? And what she truly felt was fear – skin-tingling, heart-pumping, stomach-churning fear. Not of falling out of the sky, for that would solve things, but of what was waiting for her down there – namely, the huge unknown that she was very soon going to have to face up to, alone.

Mind racing, she stared out the window. The plane must have come down a little. The sea, like a silken blue sheet, glinted up at them. That was something else from her storybooks that she'd seen now as she got further and further away from home.

It started to darken. The red wing light appeared to flash brighter as it did. Soon they were encased in night sky with only a few of Muhammed's stars hanging like sparks to keep her in his company.

She heard him again. *Towards God is the journeying, Soraya.*

Twelve

"Look at all the lights, Amir."

Soraya snapped awake.

"Mmm."

As many Amirs as Muhammeds in the world, Soraya thought, finding herself back in the plane.

"Ladies and gentlemen, we have now begun our descent into Soekarno-Hatta International Airport. In preparation for landing, please ensure that your seatbelts are fastened, your seat is in the upright position and any electronic equipment you may have is turned off. Thank you."

She watched the huge glow of Jakarta rise and pick up speed until its lights drew level, blurring past. When they hit the ground and the engines roared, she winced in discomfort, speculating that, if she could sneak back into that toilet and guide that lever into the lock position, she might be forgotten about and left there to fly back to Islamabad.

"Selamat datang di Jakarta" read a huge sign, illuminated high over a terminal building with more limbs than a centipede fastened to scores of planes, including theirs after a brief wait. Then it began in reverse: joining the end of the procession and, with no chance of slipping into a toilet, moving past the attendants and through the limbed extension into a massive building – teeming with people – without once having to go outside.

Following the flow of passengers, she searched anxiously for someone she recognised from the Islamabad bus, when a hand grabbed her shoulder. She whirled around, then wilted with relief. Looking down at her was the English-speaking Pakistani man. He smiled and held up her travel documents. How he'd got them, she had no idea.

"You must show these to the officials up ahead," he said slowly in English, placing the documents in her hand. "Do you understand?"

She nodded.

"Stay with me. I will help you."

Others followed as well.

Once past the hard-eyed officials, everyone got their bags and went down a long corridor into another crowded area.

A young man in sunglasses and rubber sandals approached. He glanced over at her, then nodded at the Pakistani as though they'd met before. "Selamat malam, bapak. Bagaimana perjalanan Bapak ke Jakarta?"

"Baik, terima kasih, Gunawan."

"Kali ini ada banyak pendatang baru. Bagus, ya?

"Ya. Tapi, harus hati-hati.

The young man glanced back over at her and continued the conversation. "Maaf, bapak. Aku mencari perempuan yang orang Afghani. Mungkin perempuan ini adalah perempuan itu. Namanya Soraya Zadran."

That was all she needed to blurt out, "I am Soraya Zadran."

"Ah." He had more to say to the Pakistani. "Kalau tiada keberatan, perempuan ini akan aku antarkan ke bus dengan beberapa pendatang baru yang lain itu."

"Sebelum berangkat, aku mau berbicara dengan dia. Sebentar saja."

"Memang saja, aku tunggu." The young Indonesian moved off a few steps and waited with his back turned.

The Pakistani took a biro and a card from his shirt pocket. "I'll be quick. My name is Rasoul Khan." He wrote a telephone number on the card and gave it to her. "If you have any problems and you need help, I want you to contact me – no one else, just me." A smile softened his stern face. "Do you understand?"

She nodded belatedly, mystified and embarrassed by the fuss. "Thank you, Mr Khan."

He extended his hand.

Strange things were already happening here. She'd never shaken a man's hand before.

*

At first, Soraya thought the mini-bus they'd taken to Islamabad had been packed on the plane, unpacked here and was now preparing to drive them away again: same size, colour, engine noise, battered appearance and blacked-out windows. But as she got on board and heard the whirring of a fan, and strange, high-pitched percussion music coming from a nearby speaker, she realised this was a different vehicle. She stepped over a plank that rattled over a hole in the aisle, and made her way to the back, where she sat next to a couple who immediately pressed themselves closer together and looked away as though she'd just stepped in dog excrement. And there she sat, alone.

Minutes later, aware of her feelings, she scolded herself. The couple were probably just as confused and scared as she was. Had she been with someone she knew, no doubt she'd have edged closer too. "Hello," Soraya said quietly, not quite getting her eyes far enough around to view them.

"Hello," the woman replied softly.

It was enough. One simple word voiced and reciprocated, and she suddenly felt better.

Interesting how fear could affect a person's view of things, Soraya thought, as the mini-bus started up and roared off to join the lights, noise and traffic of the city.

*

She'd expected a passenger ship, not more crowded alleyways and the clatter of people going up and down steps and another tiny room pinched between thin walls. At least this time the room had a dim light bulb that hung down over the mattress on the floor. There was nothing for her to do in this half-lit gloom but try to divert her mind again with English study. A brief storm rumbled in. It flashed white, cracked like gunfire and lashed her window with rain. Once it passed, she fell into a fitful sleep.

The call to prayer woke her before dawn. She had no idea which direction was west and Mecca, so she knelt, facing the window, and prayed for longer that she ever had before. Even here, in the middle of this huge city, roosters crowed in the grey light of dawn. After prayers, Soraya opened the window. The air was muggy and smelled of cooking oil, petrol and spices. The alleyway was already bustling with activity. Across from her, antennas and washing lined the rooftops. On the far horizon, black glass buildings soared up over smoke-hazy shacks, their upper levels catching the early morning sunlight.

She left the room, went out the back and joined women lined up at the concrete ablution block, like the one she and Ahmed had bickered about that first day in Aybak. There was no need for impersonations here, though. Only two women wore burqas, everyone else chadors. The women looked friendlier in the morning light. While a few quietly fingered their worry beads, others made overtures with their eyes and small smiles. Greetings and introductions followed in different languages. Three or four spoke English, including herself, after the woman she'd sat next to on the bus approached and asked how she was.

"I am fine, thank you. How are you this morning?"

The woman smiled. "I am fine too." She introduced herself as Elham. She and her husband, Salar, had come from Baghdad in Iraq.

Soraya's spirits lifted. She used her knowledge of chapter three to tell Elham where she was from and where she was going. Then it got harder. Did Elham know where Penrith, near Sydney, was? She didn't but, since she and her husband were going to a place called Marrickville, also near there, maybe they could do some things together and get to know each other better? Elham's English was good, better than Muhammed's and Amir's, perhaps as good as Rasoul Khan's. Soraya made another resolution, one she vowed to keep on penalty of being flattened by lightning – which wouldn't be difficult here. She'd get to the end of her English book by the time they arrived in Australia, then she'd go to a shop there, get an intermediate level book and practise and practise. After a few months of intense study and conversation in Penrith, she'd be up to advanced level, for sure. Wouldn't hearing about that make her family feel proud?

"Salar and I are going out to visit the markets this morning," Elham said. "Would you like to come with us?"

"Yes, thank you." The three men and now this softly-spoken, round-faced Iraqi woman. Whenever grief deepened and she was looking for a place to bury herself, it seemed Allah's guiding hand steered her into the company of another good person. Allah akbar. Hope surged. Australia wasn't far now: the place where more good people would wave and shout their greetings.

It was Soraya's turn to enter the block. "See you soon," she said to Elham.

*

A routine developed. Woken by the call to prayer, Soraya prayed, then went down and lined up outside the block, where the headscarf-framed faces had turned bright and animated.

There she practised the English she'd studied the previous night and listened for news about their departure for Australia. After sharing breakfast with Elham and Salar, they wandered through outdoor markets. Exchanging one of the American dollars her father had given her, Soraya used sign language to bargain for rice and tea, soap and vegetables. Necessities were all she could look at, she had to continually remind herself.

One day, Soraya spotted stacks of blue jeans and colourful T-shirts at a clothing stall. She watched young Indonesians rifle through the clothes, pulling out items and holding them up to each other grinning and saying things like "cool". She knew what that word meant in English. In Indonesian, she suspected it meant "good", or "great". Every T-shirt had writing across the front, some of it in English and some in Indonesian, like DON'T WORRY, BE HAPPY; I'VE BEEN TO BALI TOO; MINUMLAH COCA-COLA; I LUV JAKARTA; AKU CINTA JAKARTA; I SURVIVED THE TRAFFIC IN JAKARTA; AKU DATANG SELAMAT DARI LALU LINTAS DI JAKARTA. She counted up the number of words she knew – just twelve. But what difference did it make? Ever since she'd seen pictures of T-shirts and jeans in a magazine Khalida kept hidden away at home, she'd loved the look of them. T-shirts were much cheaper than jeans, and she longed to buy one, just to put on in her room. Maybe later, in Australia, she'd get confident enough to wear it with her chador outside. She reined in her imagination, though. Necessities, nothing else, she told herself again as young people bargained and handed over money that she couldn't begin to match for such things.

Elham approached, holding up a tiny bottle of red liquid. With a mischievous grin, she asked, "Do you know what this is?"

Soraya nodded, unable to stop grinning as well.

Elham unscrewed the top. She reached over and brushed a thin strip of polish on Soraya's thumbnail.

Instinctively, Soraya hid her thumb inside her fist, feeling Taliban eyes on her.

"For you," Elham said, replacing the top and handing her the polish.

Soraya opened her hand and gazed at her thumbnail. "Thank you."

Elham stepped over to the T-shirts and selected a light blue one with four animals and bright red lettering on it. Holding it up, her dark eyes probed Soraya's. "This one must have been traded by an Australian tourist. It would go nicely with your nail polish. Like it?" she asked, raising her voice to get over the traffic noise.

The T-shirt read, I SANG SILLY SOPRANO AT THE SYDNEY OPERA HOUSE.

Soraya recognised the kangaroo and koala, but not the sharp-beaked bird, or a bulky, stump-legged animal, or three of the words either. "Yes. It is nice." It was more than that.

"Your size, Soraya," she noted, turning to her husband.

"But, I do not have money…enough to buy it. Maybe I come back, buy it another day."

"Uh huh." Whatever silent message was exchanged between Elham and Salar, it prompted Elham to carry the T-shirt over to the stack of jeans.

A stooped, wizened old woman, in sandals and a sarong, came over. "Jins itu bermutu bagus." When Elham shook her head, the old lady said, "Jeans very good."

"Yes, I agree." Returning her attention to Soraya, Elham held up a pair of jeans. "Do you agree that these are very good?"

"Yes. But please, maybe tomorrow."

"Uh huh." As Soraya stood there, her responses ignored, Elham pressed the jeans up against her waist. "A little long, but we can shorten them. Otherwise, they'll fit perfectly."

"But..."

"Ssshh." Elham calmed her with another smile, before speaking very slowly. "In Iraq, when people meet someone they like very much and want to be friends with, the older person will often buy the younger person a gift. Usually, sometime in the future, the younger person will then buy the older person a gift in return. We Iraqis believe this ensures... uh, makes the two people stay close in each other's hearts. So in Australia, it will be your turn to buy us a gift, if you feel you want to stay close."

"I do already."

"Good."

Serious bargaining for the nail polish, T-shirt and jeans began.

*

Back in her room each day in the draining afternoon heat, Soraya repainted her nails and put on her new clothes. Her jeans felt heavy and rough at first, but her T-shirt felt great — well, what there was of it, anyway. She opened her English book and tried to study, but often fell asleep before storms came over and woke her up. After eating with Elham and Salar in the evenings, she studied until her eyes ached.

"There is comfort in habit," an Afghan woman said to her one morning.

If that was true, then her comfort level should have been brimming over. As days turned to weeks, it didn't. Nor did anyone else's.

Finally, after a squall passed over one steamy afternoon, the young man who'd met them at the airport arrived and knocked loudly on every door. "Harus siap! Must ready!" he shouted out. "Tiga jam kami berangkat! Three hour we go! Bawalah makanan serta minuman! Bring food and water!"

As excitement bubbled away in her, another knock came.

This time the door swung open and Elham popped her beaming face in. "We are going! We are going! To Australia, we are going!" she chanted, moving closer. She held Soraya by the shoulders and kissed her cheeks. "Now tell me, beautiful girl, how long will it take you to pack your things?"

Soraya's emotions stilled. *Beautiful girl.* It was what her auntie had called her just before she left Masar e-Sharif. "I think maybe ten minutes."

"Double that time for me. That gives us two hours to visit the markets. What things do you need for the trip?"

She shook her head. "Nothing. I have everything."

"Hairbrush?"

"I have a comb."

"It's windy on the sea and hairbrushes are very cheap here. You will need at least one."

"But…"

"Soraya, Westerners call it a going away present. We must now practise Western customs…uh, do what they do. So I will buy today. You can buy another day when we are together in Australia." She glanced down at Soraya's feet. "Sandals are good for around here, and your boots are good for climbing, but for a boat… Do you have shoes?"

"I don't need…"

"Walking shoes are also very cheap here. We will get some." Elham turned towards the window where drops of rain from the recent squall still dripped on the ledge. "Do you have clothes to keep you dry?"

"Please, Elham, I have enough clothes."

"You will by the time we return."

When they got back, purchases in hand, Salar already had their packs on the bus. This time, Soraya was given the window seat and Salar sat with his feet in the aisle.

"I hope the ship is not far away," Soraya commented over the noise, as the bus headed out towards the main road.

"Only about five hours the driver say to me, insha'allah," Salar replied, before adding, "once we get out of the city." He yawned, folded his arms across his chest and leaned his head back, but found nothing to support it. Elham's shoulder would have to do.

*

Another back-seat ride, but this time amidst more artificial light, people and traffic than Soraya expected to see in a lifetime. It took hours for it all to reduce to the lamplit activity of roadside stalls, headlights that flared up and flashed past, and a fat moon that reflected off the rice paddies. It was the beginning of the last stage to a new life and everyone seemed happy and inspired by that thought. The same voices she'd listened to at the ablution block each morning chirped away and laughed in front of her.

Though Salar dozed, Elham didn't. She watched the road, then later told Soraya about her son who was killed by an American missile ten years earlier, and about a cruel Iraqi leader named Saddam Hussein who'd imprisoned Salar for six years for reading American poems to his university students. "And tell me about your family, Soraya. You must miss them very much."

What they had in common was death and a shared horror of sky demons, so Soraya started there, telling Elham about her mother, before going on to the rest of her family and finishing with Muhammed and Amir.

"You're with us now," was all that Elham said after Soraya finished her story.

Road-stall lamplight and traffic thinned. Talk and laughter died away. Elham placed a hand over Soraya's and propped her head on Salar's. Without moving that hand, she fell asleep.

"God is close, Muhammed," Soraya whispered. "Don't worry, Mama. The people here are really really good to me."

Minutes later, she slept too.

*

"I don't see it."

"The water's shallow. It must be waiting for us further out."

"There, up ahead, buses. And there's a small boat with people on it. See it, Salar? It's just leaving now from the landing."

"I do, yes."

Soraya lifted her head, breathed in the salt air and looked bleary-eyed out the window at her first-ever, close up view of the sea. Three worn, high-bowed boats – each around fifteen metres in length – rested at their moorings in the middle of the small bay. People were moving over the tarpaulin-roofed deck of the one nearest the open sea. Close in, a couple of boys wading in the water turned and waved up to them. Soraya waved back. That brought smiles and shouts and more waves. Lateef's voice came to her. *They will wave and shout their greetings…* She hoped he wasn't confusing Indonesians for Australians. For the next few minutes, as they bounced and swerved past stilted houses, coconut palms and small sailing vessels that dotted the shoreline, the only other sound to disturb her thoughts was the putt – putt – putt – putt of a small, crowded boat pushing out into the bay.

Then the peace shattered. Shouts and high-pitched screams penetrated the bus. Other buses and belongings and a crowd of angry, arm-waving people began to fill the front windscreen. Inside, passengers stared and turned grim-faced. The bus shuddered to a stop on the edge of the mayhem.

The driver flung open the door and pointed in the direction of the bay. "Kapal anda, di tenggah teluknya. Sekarang anda harus berangkat dari bus ini."

No one needed a translation. Out there on the water, the small boat

83

had reached the high-bowed one nearest the open sea and people were climbing up a rope ladder to get on board.

Murmurings started. They spread and strengthened.

Someone at the front shouted out, "Where big ship for all the people?"

Moments later, the biggest shock of all hit Soraya like a sky demon. Three men stepped on the bus. The first two wore sunglasses and had guns holstered to their hips. The third man had none of those things, just the same Pakistani shirt and congenial smile he wore on the bus to Islamabad and at the airport in Jakarta.

Thirteen

Soraya tore up Rasoul Khan's card, tossed the scraps over the stern and watched them disappear into a wake that widened and flattened behind them.

The bay was gone. Other than their boat and crew, the few trailing gulls and a green strip of receding coastline were all that remained of Indonesia. Still, despite everything, she was thankful to be out here away from the screams and threats and that snake of a man, who loomed up large again in her mind.

"Congratulations!" Rasoul Khan had said earlier, scanning the people on the bus. "You are about to set off for Australia." His permanent smile widened when he spotted her at the back.

Feeling her anger rise, she stared at the floor.

"Unfortunately, as you can hear, one or two passengers are not happy about going aboard your boat and if…"

"They are not the only unhappy ones," Salar interrupted, leaning out into the aisle. His words set off more loud protests.

"No, they are not."

"The boat is too small."

"And there are too many people."

"The words were 'cruising in comfort'. That is what we were told."

Rasoul Khan held up his hand for quiet. "Please. Let me assure you that there is room for everyone on your boat. The boat is strong and your crew is very experienced. They have been to Australia many times. So please do not worry. Now, I must ask you to get your things and leave the bus." He pointed to the landing, where people continued to shout and jostle. "There is where you will board a small boat that will take you to your big, safe boat in the bay."

Some of the passengers followed his instructions, while others stayed, debating frantically.

BANG! A gunshot from the landing echoed over the water and brought stunned silence.

Rasoul Khan used the lull to his advantage. "The tide will be going out soon, and your boat will be leaving with it, so you must hurry."

A few more got their things together and left. The ones who stayed looked defiant.

As the two men flanking Rasoul Khan got out their pistols, his smile disappeared. "No one will stay on this bus. And no one will be allowed to get transport back. So you have two choices, my friends. You can swim – however, because of the sharks in the bay, nobody ever does – or you can board your boat. Please make your decision quickly."

"Let's go," Salar said.

Elham grabbed Soraya's hand and Salar picked up their things. The others did the same and moved out of the bus in front of them.

"Don't worry, be happy," Rasoul Khan called out, mimicking a market T-shirt as he helped escort them down the road to the landing. "Only a few days and you'll be in Australia."

Soraya felt as much warmth for him as she would for a Taliban executioner. Her frustration came from not being able to tell him so in English. She tried Afghani, but he ignored her. Mind-scouring her English book, she recalled a reading in chapter nine. She slowed and glared up at his deceitfully smiling face. "We are people, not animals. But don't worry, be happy and may Allah always turn away from you for what you do." For the second time that morning, Rasoul Khan lost his smile.

Had her poor mother witnessed her saying that, Soraya thought, she'd have shaken her head dismally and suffered for days. Had the Taliban witnessed it, well… Being loaded onto an old boat with a hundred and fifty people, and sent far out to sea, was light punishment compared to a whipping or a stoning. Guns and smiles, such a strange combination, she reflected, thinking again about what had happened that morning. At least the Taliban were consistent. They never smiled.

The boat vibrated now like the Peshawar trishaws had. It lifted, creaked and dropped down in the gentle swell. For a while, that was all there was, before a big sail started to flap away behind her. Two boys in oversized T-shirts and baggy shorts unfurled it and pulled hard on rope to get it up. The boat heeled over as breeze filled the sail.

She turned her eyes to the sea again and let her mind drift backwards.

I love you.

Above all else, bring honour to your mother's memory and our family.

GET THERE.

I will try to be a better mahram for you.

Towards God is the journeying, Soraya.

And that remained her greatest hope.

She told her mother again about the good people she was with, except for Rasoul Khan, of course. Elham and Salar were close by, watching the sea as well. They included her as theirs now, with their tiny bit of shared space next to the ladder down below.

Dark clouds started to bank up in great vertical columns. The sea darkened.

Never trust fat men in poor places.

Like Pervez Lateef, Soraya thought. He and Rasoul Khan – or whoever that snake really was – were obviously known to each other. Though she'd never stepped foot on a boat before, she'd once seen a picture of a comfortable passenger ship. This boat was hardly that, which added to her doubts that Australians would really be there to wave and shout their greetings. Still, they were on their way there now, weren't they? It was bad down below, but not as bad as living in a camp on the Pakistani border, or carting supplies for the Taliban. At least there was hope, and the boat journey would only last a few days. Even if Australians weren't as welcoming as Lateef said they would be, things couldn't help but be better there. Considering what the rest of her family was enduring in Afghanistan – may almighty Allah watch over them – there was little doubt who the lucky one was.

Her mind started drawing up images of her uncle's house in Penrith, and that great winged building, on that huge harbour, where so many people sang songs together.

The boat lurched in a growing swell. Wind strengthened. Spray swept over the bow and the deck got slippery. She thought about going below to get her new, waterproof clothes on, before Elham's muffled groans distracted her. Salar held on to his wife as she threw up over the side.

Minutes later, they all went below to lie down. It was wet down there and pockets of air were already thick with the smells of diesel fuel, vomit and sewage. The sea beat so hard on the hull, it was difficult to stand up or avoid crashing into people on the way to the toilet and back. To make room for her, Salar pressed closer to Elham, but Soraya shook her head and pointed upwards.

She spent the rest of the day on the main deck, before a storm came over. Rain drilled down. The sky rumbled and snapped. Below deck, water leaked through cracks in the hatch door. But the storm soon passed, and people's spirits lifted. They joined others in taking food up to the main deck, where they watched the full moon – like a great yellow egg – rise out of the sea. It found an opening through thinning clouds and cast a highway of glittering light ahead of them. There were those who speculated that it stretched as far as Australia, and they talked of it as an omen and an answer to their prayers. For everyone, the shock of the morning's events seemed to fade on the moonstruck sea. People ate. Conversation spread and brightened. Dreams were reignited.

For the next three days, the good weather held and the sea stayed calm. People used their sleeping mats as prayer mats and prayed out there. Men bunched together on the bow afterwards and placed damp towels over their heads, and chatted and smoked while scanning the horizon for Australia, until it was time to pray again or eat. The young crewmen erected the tarpaulin and women and girls in chadors and heavy dresses flocked underneath it. The girls minded young children while the women prepared meals or washed clothes, venturing out just long enough to find drying spots in the hot sun and later to retrieve what had dried. Nights turned moonless and Soraya slept on deck under Muhammed's twitching stars.

By the fifth day, people began to ration food. Women were the first not to eat.

On the morning of the sixth day, the sea paled and went completely flat, as though press-ironed by the heavy weight of the air. After lowering and furling up the mainsail, the crewmen lingered, keeping their eyes on the hot, ivory sky and talking in spasms to each other. Their edginess was catching. Families shared worried looks and worked their worry beads while eyeing the sky and water, unsure what they were looking for.

By midday, breeze rippled the water. Black clouds boiled up on the eastern sky as if signposting the lair of some fire-breathing sea monster. The boat swung round sharply, forty-five degrees. The crewmen scurried about. The tarpaulin came back down and the mainsail went back up. The engine noise strengthened and the deck vibrated hard as they picked up speed.

From the stern, Soraya could make out a strip of flashing silver that grew beside those swelling black clouds. Soon the boat rode a pitching swell. Wind began whistling in the rigging and whipped tops off the white caps. The mushrooming storm cloud caught up to them, darkening the sky. Lightning forked. Thunder rolled. Rain beat down on the deck. A wave broke over the bow, drenching Soraya and others. They dashed below. The hatch closed over them and people crashed about in the darkness as waves, like artillery shells, slammed into the hull. Some lost hold of each other and screamed out names – as if, loud enough, they might silence the storm – then groped around until they found who they were after. They clung even closer then. Parents tried to console their children but could barely be heard, nor could those who cried, prayed or vomited into the sloshing water. The air turned foul. Someone managed to strike a match and light a lantern swinging from a crossbeam. A few found torches, and blades of light pierced the blackness, illuminating the chaos and panic and the crack in the hull where water spouted in like a tilted fountain.

Minutes later, water began gushing through. Men shouted instructions. Buckets and cooking pots were found. Salar staggered up the ladder and nudged the hatch door open. Lightning flashed white and water streamed down the opening like liquid metal. While women held the torches and their shrieking children, men organised themselves into teams and began bailing furiously, passing the containers up to Salar.

The storm raged on all night as though they were its chosen enemy. The boat jerked, plunged and shook. The hull groaned and made terrible wrenching noises. People shouted and wailed. In a crossbeam of torchlight, a terrified mother held her young son over her head and stared at him as if saying goodbye.

At dawn, the storm suddenly quit, and within minutes the sea went perfectly still again, exhausted as well. Just the low sobs of a few children and water trickling in through the hull disturbed the silence, before the two crewmen came down and surveyed the damage.

"Keluar! Get out!" one shouted, his voice a whip to get people moving again.

When the crewmen returned to wedge fabric into the crack and hammer a piece of board over it, no one had left.

They both tried again. "Keluar! Keluar!"

Passengers looked around hollow-eyed and continued to wallow in the water. Only when sunlight broke through and steam began rising off the main deck, did they start to move. It took nearly an hour for everyone to get themselves and their wet, smelly belongings out into the fresh air. There they prayed, slept and dried their things. No one ate.

So dazed were they that they failed to notice a ship bearing down on them from astern, until a loudspeaker blared out, "This is HMAS *Hobart*. You are in Australian territorial waters and are hereby ordered to stop and prepare for a boarding party. I repeat, this is HMAS *Hobart*..."

The engine slowed to an idle. The boat ceased vibrating and leaned over to one side as people rushed to watch the ship move up beside them, about fifty metres away. Two small boats were launched with a dozen men in uniforms, red caps and life vests. In minutes, they were alongside, hoisting ladders over the gunwhales and climbing on board.

"Asylum," a few English-speaking passengers shouted out in quick succession.

Some smiled and waved to the Australians. Others followed up with greetings.

"Good morning to you. So happy to see you."

"Hello. We are refugees. We love Australia."

"We've just been through a terrible storm," Elham said to a stout, short-bearded man who stood next to her.

He ignored her.

Soraya's eyes followed the eyes of others studying the Australians. No waves, no smiles, just duty-bound vigilance as the navy men kept their feet wide spread and their hands clasped in front of them. Like Rasoul Khan's men, they also carried pistols on their hips. Soraya's stomach grew cold as wide-eyed passengers around her went quiet and drew closer together.

Two Australians with gold epaulets on their shoulders consulted in front of them.

"We are going to Australia, yes?" an Iraqi man at the back yelled out.

No reply.

"Yes?" the man tried again, his voice ringing out louder in the nagging silence.

"Yes," came a flat reply from the front.

The tension broke. Excitement surged. People embraced. "Australia! Australia!" many began chanting, wrapping their arms around each other and performing a dance step or two. A few lifted their raw eyes and palms to the sky and shouted, "Allah akbar! Allah akbar!" while others knelt down and gave thanks in prayer.

The boarding party broke up. Two went towards the deckhouse, where the grim-faced captain and crew awaited them. Four others began inspecting the deck and the hold below. The remaining six took out biros and small notebooks and asked people who spoke English to come forward and translate. Over the next few hours, as information was collected, joyful passengers pressed up close to the Australians, smiling and laughing and eager to help.

Once lines were attached to their bow and the Australians had returned to their ship, the boat was towed slowly on. On deck, people continued to celebrate by sharing the last of their food and talking about what life was going to be like in such a peaceful, prosperous land.

Fourteen

"Allow me to welcome you again to Woomera. You're finished checking in now, so if you'll be kind enough to follow me, I'll show you to your barracks." The bulky guard shook his head as if clearing it. "Sorry. The word's 'quarters'. I'll show you to your quarters," he corrected himself in a jaunty voice, while escorting them and an Uzbek Afghani family over the gravel to a long, low rectangular building glinting in the sun like all the others. "I dare say your lodgings here will be a step up from your recent standard of accommodation. Much in demand by our overseas visitors is our Oscar Compound, positioned, as it is, just a short distance from our picturesque main gate and offering, as you'll no doubt agree after passing a few seasons with us here, the finest outback views south of the Alice."

Elham and Salar were the only ones who caught the irony in what he was saying. "It would be better, I think, if you did not say these things to us," Salar said.

The guard stopped and took off his mirror sunglasses to get a closer look at Salar. "Do you, now? Right, as you wish, number one eighty-four. I wouldn't want your first day here to be anything less than rewarding."

Utterly bewildered by what was happening, Soraya lagged behind.

The guard glanced back at her. "Better move it along," he shouted. "You'll end up getting lost back there."

Lost. A chapter ten word. She used it in a silent sentence: I got lost in a place called Darwin before I got here. When Elham looked around for her, extending her hand, Soraya hurried to catch up.

*

On the third day, Soraya located a bench at the back of the prison. She brushed the grit off it and sat down. Staring out through the bars at the empty earth and sky, she heard her mother again. *Why were you born so contrary? Born to continually question?* She felt those thin arms embrace her. "I'm sorry," Soraya whispered. Hopelessness closed in. What use was memory, anyway? No amount of remembering could change anything or bring people back. A rush of tears came. How surprising, she thought, facetiously. She decided against wiping them away. What was the point? No one was around, and watching them drop and disappear into the dry earth gave her something to do.

*

Their room was small. They shared it with the Uzbek Afghani family, whose two young sons cried much of the night and insisted on staying in bed during the day.

Later, two angry Iraqi men were moved in next to them. The men were often in trouble and handcuffed for hours at a time.

One day, after another loud encounter with guards, the younger one stormed in and made a point of rolling up his left sleeve and showing Soraya his arm. "Do you know what this word says in English?" he ranted.

It was the same word cut into his arm three times.

"Freedom," she answered, slightly sickened.

"Do you know what the word means?"

She welcomed the opportunity to get away from him. "I can get my English dictionary and…"

He grabbed her by the arm. "I don't need it." His eyes bored into her. "Just answer these questions Yes or No for me."

She was too scared not to. "Okay."

"One: does freedom mean being sent to a desert prison for going into another country and asking for help?"

She gazed at the floor. It obviously did in this country. "No," she answered.

"Two: does freedom mean having to ask guards to unlock gates and doors so you can go eat?"

93

"No, but the food is good," she muttered, hoping to divert him.

He only heard what he wanted to. "Three: does freedom mean not being told how long you are going to be forced to stay in a desert prison?"

"No." She thought then that she'd start spending more time on the bench at the back.

He stopped and stared at her, perhaps realising for the first time the anguish he was causing her. His anger eased. His face softened. "Freedom is also not being forced to answer questions you don't want to." He rolled his sleeve down, turned and walked away.

*

Nights closed in quickly and grew longer. Resentment peaked then. People bickered and quarrels broke out. Children wet their beds and blamed their parents. Wives blamed their husbands. Husbands fled outside into the cold and screamed at the lights overhead. Others screamed too. An Iranian girl drank a bottle of shampoo. Her mother ran outside screaming for help. An ambulance arrived and took them away.

An Iraqi woman slashed her wrists late one night. Her husband screamed carrying her outside as women tried frantically to wrap her wounds. When the ambulance came, the man was sedated as well and driven away with his wife.

Riots tended to occur the day after a night of screaming.

*

Elham and Salar started sharing the bench with her. If she wasn't at a male-delivered hygiene lecture with other women, or in conference with Mike, a friendly, slow-talking lawyer, Soraya would sit with them and stare out at the desert. The silence out there was powerful. It absorbed lingering screams and frustrations if you watched and listened long enough. So they rarely disturbed that silence, even by praying. If Muhammed was right – that towards God was the journeying – then God was lost to them here.

What they could hear on the bench – when distant shouting didn't intrude – was the cawing of crows, the rumble of trucks from an unseen highway and wind that occasionally whipped up dust devils like it did outside Masar e-Sharif that first day.

Later, they watched the sun sink in a blaze of gold, while in the east the Earth's pale blue shadow lifted over the razor wire into a darkening sky. As Muhammed's stars appeared, growing in number and brightness, Woomera's glow of nightlights arced up replacing the earth shadow. Sound was reduced to the trucks then, their headlights flicking out across the far-flung darkness.

*

She'd been to the town of Woomera. She'd travelled the two kilometres there on a bus with other children to attend school in a room at the back of a white Christian church. The town was beautiful, like an oasis dropped out of the sky. Big houses with sloping roofs – surrounded by trees and colourful plant life – lined the smooth, clean roads. Cars powerful enough to drag smaller houses, mounted on wheels, glided up and down those roads. A frightening display of planes and sky demons occupied the centre of town, along with glass-walled shops, a huge fountain and women pushing babies around in small carts.

One day, outside the classroom, Soraya took special notice of a nearby pale brick wall. It stood as high as the prison's fences and had a colourful mural of the prophet Jesus in a white robe encircled by smiling children with many different skin colours and clothing styles. At the top of the mural was a caption that said, "LET THE CHILDREN COME TO ME. DO NOT STOP THEM, BECAUSE THE KINGDOM OF HEAVEN BELONGS TO SUCH AS THESE."

There were no guards or fences in the mural. And she wondered whereabouts in Australia such a place could be. So she asked Elham when she returned.

"It's nowhere in Australia." Elham replied. "It's a lie."

Soraya refused to go to classes in that small room after that. Instead, she spent more time on the bench with Elham and Salar staring out at the desert.

*

"One hundred and eighteen big steps," Soraya said one morning. Numbers were, after all, a common language here. "From the nearest edge of the main compound," she went on, "it's that far to the bench here."

At one time, Elham would have shown interest. "Oh," she uttered, gazing out at the emptiness.

With her eyes still raw from tear-gas, Soraya spent the previous day stepping off distances from where those Iraqi men from her Oscar Compound had impaled themselves in razor wire. "This is a good place, Elham. But it is cold in the early morning without the sun. So if you want, we can sit on the other side before breakfast," she said, anxious to cater to Elham in any way she could.

Elham's voice stayed flat. "No. Here is fine."

"Okay."

*

With his arms and hands heavily bandaged, Ehsan – the Iraqi who had carved the word freedom on his arms and later jumped onto razor wire – joined them on the bench. At midday, when the sun arrived, if things were quiet they'd take a walk to view the new arrivals in the main compound or check to see if Australians had gathered on the outer perimeter. If a sizeable number of Australians had, prisoners often tried it again – unveiling placards, hurling themselves at fences, climbing up on the hot metal rooftops and screaming appeals. But not number six seventy-one, not Ehsan – not any more. The first sign of trouble now, and he led them back to their bench, one hundred and eighteen big steps away from the rioting.

*

Guards in crisp white shirts and dark blue trousers walked past at regular intervals.

"Everything up to your expectations here?" the Welcome to Woomera man often asked, not bothering to wait for a reply. "Splendid. You will let me know if you require anything? You know, like the supermarket ads, stock market reports, real estate guide, the usual sorts of things."

Though Elham and Salar didn't agree, Soraya thought he only said those things out of boredom and needed to joke to people. Other guards were either indifferent, or friendly and considerate when they could afford to be. They nodded their greetings and prompted conversations at times.

One day, a new guard – tall and thin, with a droopy red moustache – stopped and eyed the closed English book on Soraya's lap. "That's a fine lookin' book ya have there. My name's Sean. What're yours?" he asked them with a lilt in his voice.

Soraya remembered the last person who'd smiled like that at her. *Congratulations. You are about to set off for Australia… Don't worry, be happy.* And after living on his and Pervez Lateef's promises, here she was. So nowadays she was wary of non-prisoner smiles. "Numbers one eighty-four, one eighty-five and one eighty-six," she answered, continuing to stare through the fence.

Sean never passed by after that without saying something. "Ya know, as a young lad, m'father came out ta this country on a boat," he started chatting away one afternoon. "After the war, it was – the Second World War, that is. Anything but a luxury liner that one was. Nonetheless, it was silver service compared ta a few that've landed on our northern shores in recent times… M'father was from the ol' country – Ireland, that is. Have ya ever heard of the place?"

They stayed silent, their eyes fixed on the horizon.

It didn't seem to bother him, though. He appeared content to stand there talking to himself. "Right. Well I might mention a few more of Ireland's geographical details when next I'm by. We Irish have a habit of doin' that, ya know."

A few chat stops later, Sean leaned back against the fence and read

Soraya's T-shirt. "I sang silly soprano at the Sydney Opera House." He chuckled. "I love it. Where can I get one?"

"In Jakarta," Elham answered.

"At an open market," Salar added.

"Would you take us with you?" Elham followed up.

Sean suffered a mood change. "I see… Well, if I could, I…" For the first time, he ran out of words, and moved on.

*

"Good mornin'." He took off his sunglasses and leaned forward. His eyes were big and as blue as the open sky. "The name's Sean. Ya remember that, don't ya? Or Irish Sean Donovan ta those I take a likin' ta, like you. I wouldn't mind knowin' your name."

He was certainly persistent. She couldn't hold out any more. "My name is Soraya."

"That's a lovely name. I still like your T-shirt."

"I know you do." Tears came to her eyes and she had to look away. "Thank you."

"Indeed, you're welcome." He looked up and down the fence line, before coming closer. "Listen, that lawyer, the one who I saw ya with yesterday afternoon in the interview room, he's as fine a bloke as you're ever likely ta meet. If anyone can do the right thing by ya, it'll be him."

Thinking how different Sean was to the other guards – especially the Welcome to Woomera man – Soraya's eyes fixed on the horizon. She decided to confide in him. "He is trying to find out where my uncle is."

Elham's wall of silence cracked, as if she'd made the same decision. "And he said something about a temporary protection visa. But we still don't understand what that is."

"Well, basically, it's what people need ta get outta here. Listen, I'll speed up my round, be back soon, then try ta explain what it is ta ya as clearly as I can."

"Thank you."

Sitting across the white-top table from Mike the lawyer, Soraya wondered whereabouts in Australia he lived. It couldn't be anywhere near here, she'd long since decided, because he seemed uncomfortable in the heat and was easily distracted by the flies. Despite that, his earnest eyes, friendly manner and the slow, considerate way he talked to her made her think he was a good man. He was the first Australian she'd learned to trust – Irish Sean Donovan being the second.

This was Mike's fourth visit and all his usual questions about her life here had been asked, so it was time to hear what he'd really come to say. After waving a pesky fly away, a look of dismay passed over his face. He leaned closer. "We know, don't we, Soraya, that your uncle is no longer living in Penrith, New South Wales, and that there is strong evidence… You understand that word now?

"Yes."

"There is strong evidence to suggest he's somewhere in south-east Queensland." He lifted his palms in the air. "But where, exactly, I still don't know."

She nodded and spoke the next three words fluently, but with little energy, "Temporary protection visa?"

He folded his hands, his eyes fastened on the table. "If I can locate your uncle, then there might be a chance you can get one, especially now that…"

She waited.

He looked up, still troubled. "In your country, with all its problems, children have to grow into adults very quickly, isn't that right?"

"Yes."

"You're fifteen, an adult. I want you to know that part of what I have to say, I wouldn't say to a child… I have both good news and bad news for you. Two days ago, in response to a request I made, I received a phone call from the Afghani Embassy…uh, important Afghani people in Canberra, our capital city. They told me your brother Ahmed has been found. He's in Masar e-Sharif with your relatives." Seeing her face light up, he paused to let her savour the good news. "But sadly, there's more that I must tell you. I've also been told that your father was killed several months ago in the fighting around Masar e-Sharif. I'm sorry, Soraya."

*

"Still claiming our own little piece of Woomerastan back here, I see."

Soraya peered up and saw her face reflected in the Welcome to Woomera man's mirror sunglasses. She ignored him and stared back out at the desert where nothing moved but the heat and flies and mirages that danced on the horizon, before disappearing like her dreams of Australia.

"Ready to set the world alight again this morning, are we? If so, there's a bit of action building up on the other side, if you're interested. You know the sort of thing, television cameras and journo-jockeys whipping up the voices of the university weekender set." He turned to Ehsan. "This might be the time to resurrect your celebrated razor-wire trampolining skills and see yourself back on the evening news in rooftop, free-fall mode again."

Ehsan might as well have been earless, sitting as straight and still as the spiked steel bars in front of them, which, judging by his appearance, held far more interest for him than the Welcome to Woomera man.

"Little call for stitched lips amongst you lot, is there?" He squeezed past them. "Anyway, I can't get bogged down here discussing worldly issues. Must press on and see what career moves our guests further along have conjured up." He seemed to be talking more to himself than them. "It's always a delight talking to you. Do have a nice day."

*

"FREEDOM! FREEDOM! FREEDOM!"

Night screams had been long and loud, so at first they discounted the build-up of placard-waving, fence-shaking racket as being just what the Welcome to Woomera man said it was – a predictable "bit of action".

100

But when a large mass of demonstrators began forming up outside – screaming and waving placards as well – they realised it was going to be more than that.

"FREEDOM! FREEDOM! FREEDOM!"

As the four of them moved into the main compound, dozens of prisoners ran past screaming and joining the protest, which soon turned into a riot. The riot grew and spread fast, echoing over the desert.

Guards formed a tight cordon and tried to drive a wedge through the rioters, who stood their ground fighting and hurling objects, before water cannon opened up on them.

Ignoring outnumbered police, demonstrators surged forward and latched on to the main gate and fence screaming, "FREEDOM! FREEDOM! FREEDOM!"

Iron bars the size of oars banged away at the fence, then poked through and began prying away at the bars. "PULL! PULL! PULL!"

When police yanked demonstrators off the fence and dragged them away, other demonstrators took their places.

"PULL! PULL! PULL!" The bars bent slowly.

Chants turned to cheers as two prisoners squeezed through and ran off.

Tear gas rose and fell as thick vapour trails.

"RUN!" Elham screamed as it drifted their way.

Soraya raced off, then, realising she was alone, stopped. "Elham! She spun round. "Elham!" Gas enveloped her, sending tears streaming down her face. "Elham!" She ran back, knocking into people. "Elham!"

Someone gripped her from behind and shoved her towards a breach in the fence. Blurred demonstrators were there – wild-eyed, red-faced, their mouths shrieking.

Jelly-like hands reached in. Close voices appealed to her, "C'mon! Get out! Get out! We'll help you!" One hand – with silver rings shimmering on every finger – gripped hers and yanked her through the bars. More cheers rang out. The hand stayed. "Run!" the girl implored, pulling her hard across the open ground.

Fifteen

"Go Sam! Go! Go! Go!" the girl screamed, still holding on to Soraya's hand in the back seat. The engine roared. Gravel machine-gunned the undercarriage. They slid sideways in a cloud of road dust before the tyres gripped, launching them forward.

"We've got lift-off!" Sam shouted.

Veering right, they sped through the open main gate and out onto the road, where they swept up on big cars pulling small houses and swerved around them so fast that, when Soraya spun around, the cars were like flies on the back windscreen.

"Oooeee!" Adorned in nose studs, earrings, finger rings and bangles, the thin, yellow-haired girl in the front banged the dashboard and chanted, "We've got freedom, freedom, freedom!" before shooting a hand up in the air. Sam did the same and their hands snapped forward meeting in a loud smack. "Oooeee!" they chorused, before the girl shouted out over the engine, "That was awesome! Let's hear it from the back, Leah! Like, what was it again?" She swirled around and offered up both hands in expectation.

"Awesome!" the attractive Leah hooted, slapping the outstretched hands.

"Incredible!"

"Unbelievable!"

Loud, throbbing music blared out from surrounding speakers.

Passing a road train, the two girls went suddenly mute, gazing at Soraya, who sat stilled in shock.

"Hi. I'm Leah," said the one next to her.

"And I'm Sarah."

"And I'm Michael Schumacker, alias Sam!" the cap-wearing driver shouted, adjusting his sunnies and glancing back at her in the rear-view mirror.

Failing to get a response, Leah tried again. "That's an awesome T-shirt you've got on." She straightened up and pulled her shoulders back so Soraya could get the full view of the one she was wearing. "You like mine?" – IF YOU THINK I'M A BITCH, YOU SHOULD SEE MY MOTHER, it read.

There was only one word Soraya couldn't understand, but she assumed it must mean beautiful person, because Leah was. "Yes. It is very nice."

Leah stifled a smirk. "Yeah, well…like, there've been other comments made, the most polite being, 'No thanks. I'd rather drop off a cliff.' But I think I prefer yours. What's your name?"

That word must mean something else, Soraya decided, nerve-wracked.

Another road train whooshed past going in the opposite direction.

"My name is Leah. What is your name?" Leah persisted, more slowly.

Whether all this would turn into a dream or a nightmare, one thing was certain. Other than military people, the guards and Mike the lawyer, these were the only Australians she'd ever met and they weren't anything like what she expected. Trying hard to calm herself, she gave them her name.

"Oooeee!" Sam's palms beat the steering wheel. "Top name! Where ya from, Sore-ya?"

She'd never been in such a vehicle, and never seen anything, other than a plane, that travelled so fast. "I am from Afghanistan."

"Well, welcome to Australia!" he shouted out even louder over the music and engine noise.

"Thank you."

Sarah gave her a reassuring smile. "You must be going bananas after all that's happened. No worries, you'll be right. Like we're students from Adelaide University and we're members of the Coalition for the Protection of Asylum Seekers against Deportation." She caught her breath. "Like thousands of others in this country, we believe in freedom, not prisons, for asylum seekers and refugees who come here needing our help. Like you."

"Oh." Soraya recalled Ehsan ranting about these things months earlier. She ran *believe in freedom, not prisons and needing our help* through her mind again. Maybe the dream was about to start, she allowed herself to think briefly.

Leah swept her long dark hair back over her shoulders and leaned closer. "Like, Sarah and I have got a flat in Adelaide," she explained, "where you can stay until things die down and we can like…do things to help you start a new life here. Can't we, Sarah?"

"Yeah, no worries." Sarah shifted around to face the front and lowered the music.

Their moods settled, their voices dropped. Soraya's fears eased.

"So whadaya think about staying at our flat, then?" Leah queried, still bright-faced.

This time, Soraya decided to ask about a word she didn't understand – how it was used, anyway. "Please. Could you tell me what 'flat' means?"

"Yeah. It has two meanings. But 'flat', the noun, means a place to live, like a small house," Leah answered, as a teacher would to a student.

"Thank you."

"No worries. Like, a couple of weeks in our flat should do it, don't ya think, Sarah?"

"Should do."

"Right, now that that's been decided," Sam said loudly, adrenalin still running hot in his veins, "it's about time to contact base and tell 'em we've got cargo."

Sarah picked up a small wireless phone and began pushing buttons. "Terry," she said into it, "Sarah here, announcing a Woomera protest like no other in history. There are, like, I don't know, maybe a dozen or so who're out, including Soraya, age about fifteen, I'd say, from Afghanistan. We're heading your way with her right now at just under 747 pace." Listening, a slow grimace contorted her face. She met Sam's flicking eyes. "You're joking!" she exclaimed. "Yeah. Okay, right. I'll ring back." She pressed a button and lowered the phone. "Police road block about fifty ks north of Port Augusta."

Sam braked and his mood quickly turned to concern. "Jesus! Didn't waste any time, did they?" The car jerked over to the side of the road and skidded to a stop. "Time for a gear change, and I'm not talking cars. And Sarah, when you're finished, ring Josh and see what's happening up north."

From a large bag under her feet, Leah handed Soraya a wide-brimmed hat, frayed jeans and a long-sleeve shirt. "Don't worry about the hat yet. Just put the jeans and shirt on for now." She tossed more hats, clothes and pairs of sunglasses up to the front seat before stripping off her shorts and T-shirt in full view of everyone.

Soraya sat there dumbfounded.

"Go on," Leah coaxed her. "Don't be scared. It's called a disguise. Like, in case the…" Her voice caught. "Like, it's just better to wear these sorts of clothes out here," she said, losing her enthusiasm for the first time.

Soraya locked her eyes on the back of Sam's head and shook her head. "I cannot."

"What?" The penny dropped seconds later. "Oh right, I see. Sam, would you mind going outside and checking the tyres for a minute?" Leah asked.

He shot his head round. "What? Whadaya on about?" When Leah glanced over and nodded at Soraya, he got the message. "Oh, yeah, right."

"And could you take your new wardrobe out there with you?"

"Yeah, yeah," he grumbled, climbing out. "Be quick. We're copper fodder out in the open here."

Sarah went back on the phone. "Josh. Sarah." This time she skipped the preliminaries. "We've got a special passenger, and there's a road block further south. What's it…" She didn't get the chance to finish. She called out to Sam, "Three other cars with refugees got through up north, but now there's a road block up – like, just outside Wirraminna."

"Right, try Tim."

In the confined space, Leah struggled with Soraya's frozen joints to get the jeans and shirt on her. When she did, she stuffed her scarf, T-shirt and Afghani dress under the driver's seat. "Now you look like a real Aussie," Leah told her, looking back up and grinning encouragement.

"Oh."

"I'll get back, Josh." Sarah hung up, threw the jeans and shirt over what she had on and used the phone again. "Tim. Sarah. There're road blocks north and south on the Stuart Highway. What's happening there?" She listened, frowning, then called out to Sam again. "A police car's on the side of the Roxby Downs road – like, not far from the Andamooka junction – but the track to Andamooka's clear. Tim can swap at the Woomera Bush Cemetery. Know where that is?"

Sam ducked his head in. "Yeah, where dead grandparents go, not far off the highway. The problem is, after Andamooka that track goes nowhere."

"Got any other ideas?"

"Not at the moment. That'll have to do. Tim's got a warehouse of camping gear in the four-wheel drive, so we can bush camp then check out the copper tide in the morning. Hopefully, it'll be out. Tell him we'll be there in half an hour. Okay to occupy my seat again, ladies?"

"Yeah, fine," Leah said, as Sarah got back on the phone to Tim.

They sped off, hanging a hard U-turn and heading back where they came from.

Reaching cruising speed in seconds and levelling off, Sam glanced in the rear-view mirror. "Coppers!" he shouted, slowing the car back down. "Get that hat on her quick, Leah!"

Leah did, while a hush fell over everyone. They sat still as stone and stared straight ahead, too scared to look round.

With their red and blue roof lights flashing, two police cars streaked past them just as the township of Woomera reappeared on their right.

"Watch which way they go," Sam said, as they started to pick up speed again.

A minute later, the police cars passed the Roxby Downs/Andamooka turn-off and veered left towards the detention centre.

Tensions eased. Spirits lifted.

"Beauty!" Sam responded, slapping the steering wheel again and turning off in the opposite direction. "Start getting things ready, happy campers. Four-wheel drive rendezvous time eighteen minutes and counting."

Glowing again, Leah asked, "How's the hat feel?"

"Very good," Soraya lied, forcing a smile.

"Excellent. After sleeping out tonight, we'll get into Adelaide tomorrow, no worries. So everything'll turn out fine. Like, all you've gotta do now is sit back and relax. Easy."

Impossible. She might as well have been told to walk back to Afghanistan.

*

It was what she could do better than them and it calmed her being able to do it. Judging by their mesmerised looks, it had the same effect on them as they sat on rocks watching flames leap into the night before eventually lowering to coals. Soraya again asked for their permission, this time to correctly place the cooking pots of chicken soup, noodles and dried vegetables on rocks over the fire. After everything was arranged, they complimented her and asked where she'd learned such skills.

"My mother teach me, also my friend Muhammed," she replied, before glancing up at his stars and absorbing the stillness. In those brief moments, she heard her mother again and saw Mustafa and Muhammed there in the circle with them, reflections of the campfire dancing in their eyes also.

"Who's Muhammed?" Leah asked for the three of them.

Soraya cut straight to the rooftop of their Kabul bus as they climbed into the mountains that day. She described everything that happened. Their one-word interjections grew in number and volume when she told them about Muhammed – her rohani – and how he'd guided her through his mountains to Pakistan.

"Wow."

"Awesome."

"Incredible."

The ringing of a phone in the four-wheel drive broke the spell and ended her story.

Sam grabbed a torch and disappeared to answer it. Just him, responding in monosyllables, before he returned, sat down and stared at the cooking pots and coals again. "Tim," he said, without shifting his gaze. "The three of 'em are in under the big tent at the Woomera Caravan Park. It seems a police and media convention is going on around them."

"So we don't go that way tomorrow," Sarah noted, stating the obvious.

"Not unless we want to be part of it."

Leah took the soup off the fire and poured it in plastic bowls. "That leaves the Roxby Downs road…if it's clear."

She passed soup and spoons around to everyone. Then Soraya helped her serve up the rice and vegetables.

"Apparently, according to Tim," Sam piped up moments later, "the other big news item is our illustrious Minister for Big Business and Prisons has gone on the box to say he'll be, like, introducing yet another clause into the country's asylum seeker penal laws."

"And pray, what would that be?" Sarah asked, mimicking the royal family.

"Ten years' imprisonment for anyone caught helping escapees."

Soraya felt everyone's eyes turn her way.

Stunned, Sarah played herself now. "So we can join them behind bars now, can we?"

"You reckon our favourite minister is this year's front-runner for the Nobel Prize's humanitarian award, Leah?"

"For sure. Like, all bets are off."

"Please. That word 'escapee.' What does it mean?" Soraya asked Leah.

"An escapee is a person who escapes or gets free from a prison."

"So I am escapee?"

"Yes." She patted Soraya's hand. "No worries. Like, there's no more they can possibly do to you, is there?"

"But to you?"

Leah smiled and tried to sound upbeat. "Just empty threats. Like, it won't happen."

Soraya looked over at the other two. Their glum faces told a different story. Reprimanding herself for thinking this could be the start of her dream, she dropped her head and bit back her sorrow.

"Got any assignments due next week?" Leah asked Sarah.

"A Psychology one on Tuesday."

"Can you get an extension?"

"Yeah, I spose I'll have to…like, whenever we get back."

"What about you, Sam?"

"No. The slate's clear till the following week."

"I've got an English Lit one due like on Friday."

They went silent. Soraya watched them as they ate hunched over, sharing their real thoughts with the fire. If there was one thing she'd learned a lot about since leaving Masar e-Sharif, it was how to read moods and detect evasiveness and dishonesty in people. It wasn't difficult to do with these three. Already they'd had enough. Their adventure had turned into something they hadn't counted on. Following that latest phone conversation, they felt trapped and scared. Who could blame them? And who could blame them also for wanting to return to their normal lives again? Which they could do if…

A long, quavering howl pierced the night. Heads snapped up.

Only Sam remained unfazed. "Just a dingo. No dramas."

"Gotta smoke, Sam?" Sarah asked, looking uncomfortable.

"Domestic or imported?"

"Surprise me."

He looked up at the half-moon and stars. "Like, would something exotic, mildly mood-enhancing to complement this awesome night meet with your satisfaction?"

"Oooo. You read my mind."

"Care to partake, Leah?" Sam asked, taking out a small plastic bag from his coat pocket.

"Like, is our favourite minister xenophobic?"

"Happy campers prison-phobic?" Sarah chimed in, barely able to emit a feeble laugh.

The others stayed quiet.

Soraya finished eating, then picked up the soup pot and asked, "Is there soap and water for washing things with?"

"Yeah," Sam replied. "Wait a sec." He pinched a length of tobacco from the plastic bag onto a small strip of white paper, rolled and sealed it with his tongue before passing her the torch. "They're in a box, at the back. The soap's called detergent." He spelled the word for her. "Give me a hoy if you can't find it."

"Thank you." In the wavering torchlight, she spotted a large rock close to their vehicle. She went over and pried it up. Perfect, she decided. This was where she'd lie down after explaining to the others how much she liked sleeping out in the open, how much it reminded her of Muhammed. With their tent set up close to the fire, she'd be a good distance away from them.

She returned to the vehicle and turned her attention to what was in the back. Lots, fortunately. She located the detergent then kept rummaging around. A wave of discomfort hit her as she collected another torch, a full water bottle, rice, bread, tea bags, a box of matches, a small knife and a backpack to put everything into. She'd lose a hand if she were caught doing this by the Taliban, she thought, before spotting a pen next to a folder of paper. She picked up the pen, carefully took a sheet of paper from the folder and wrote a note.

Dear my frends Sam, Leea and Saira
    Thank you.
    I do not want you to come to prison. So you not to wory I go back to Woomera now so you can go to your home.
    I am sorry but I boro a little bit for my trip back. When I get more monee I send more to you at Adelay Universitee for these things.
    I remember you.
    Your frend,
    Soraya

She had all her money – twenty-five dollars – in her dress under the seat. She'd place the note and ten dollars on the front windscreen as she was leaving, probably in an hour or two, as she'd be too nervous to sleep until she was well away from here.

"Find it all right?" Sam shouted out.

"Yes, I find it now, thank you."

"Like, don't go mistaking the detergent for the brake fluid," he said, giggling.

The others giggled with him.

It was good they were starting to feel better, Soraya thought. "No. It says…" She spelled that d word out for him.

"Awesome."

"Mmm, incredible."

"Faaaaantastic."

After getting her clothes out and gathering everything up, she went over to the rock, lifted it up and placed the full daypack underneath it. Setting the rock down and kicking dirt up around its edges completed the task. She was ready now to wish them goodnight.

Sixteen

A fly buzzed, ending her dream. The top of her head felt warm as though it was next to a campfire. No hissing, no crackling, no smell of smoke, though. Just that single fly – there one moment, gone the next – followed by a stillness so deep she thought she was back in the mountains with Muhammed.

Her eyes cracked open. She peeked out over the top of her sleeping bag at the rolling landscape, not recognising it at first. Startled, she propped on her elbows and let her mind catch up to this patch of gently rising ground – bordered in torchlight just hours earlier, a mere speck under a huge open sky now.

Muhammed's voice rose in her mind. *Towards God is the journeying, Soraya.*

Mecca, the birthplace of the prophet Mohammed, was surrounded by land like this: land that the prophet wandered over almost fifteen hundred years ago, receiving revelations from Allah, then teaching and converting people. Moslems still wandered these deserts, still considered them divine places. And for the first time since leaving the boat, Soraya felt like praying. Holding the worn sleeping bag around her against the cold, she got to her knees, turned away from the rising sun and touched her forehead to the red earth in prayer.

Fut – fut – fut – fut – fut – fut – fut… Her nightmare returned.

She glanced up, suddenly trembling.

Fut – fut – fut – fut – fut… Behind her, skimming low and getting closer.

Memory took over. Afghanistan. Tat – tat – tat – tat – tat… Gunfire raked the ground. Whoosh. Whoosh. Rockets streaked to the valley floor. Muhammed's voice was in her ear. It's far away, Soraya, not here, not here.

Images of that valley free-flowed through her mind as she jerked her head around and squinted into the sun trying to locate the helicopter again. Fut – fut – fut – fut…

Grabbing the backpack and pressing it tightly against her, she burrowed back down into the sleeping bag. There she stayed, perfectly still, listening to her heartbeat and that helicopter as it veered left towards the dirt road. Moments later, it seemed to hover. She peered out again and spotted it descending close to where the campsite had to be, before it disappeared behind a rise. Police? Who else could it be? They'd question Sam, Sarah and Leah, who'd say nothing for fear of going to prison for ten years. But what if the police spotted something – like her note or her footprints that would extend to the side of that road she'd walked on? Scrambling out of the sleeping bag, she packed up quickly and made a dash for a jagged rock outcrop further up the slope. There she hid, watched and waited.

As the helicopter lifted back into view, a rising streamer of road dust began tracking towards Woomera. It wasn't long before a vehicle – looking dwarfed out there – emerged into clear space. At first it moved in the same direction as the helicopter. Minutes later, though, the helicopter banked right and flew over a ridge of red sand, before its thumping rotor blades gradually faded away. Utter silence returned. They couldn't know, Soraya decided. She sat up and watched that dust streamer getting smaller and smaller in the distance.

*

His eyes would go all huge seeing her. A smirk would cut across his face and he might say something like "Welcome back to Woomera. Lovely to see you again. And how was your time away?" What were some of the other words he'd used? Ah yes. "Restful and relaxing, was it? Thirsty work though, being out there in all that open heat and sand and glare. But never mind. Once bitten, twice shy." Elham had explained to her what that meant. "Time moves on. So is everything moving along to your satisfaction now that you're back with us again?"

There was one good thing about having to listen to the Welcome to Woomera man – it improved her English, but not to the point where she was prepared to endure all that again. Besides, ten years for helping someone escape would mean at least that much prison time for the person who did the escaping. So, as there was no chance of getting her temporary protection visa until she was at least in her mid-twenties, if then, what was the point in following the direction of that road dust back to Woomera? At least if she died out here, it would be with dignity and pride. And if the pain and suffering became too great, the knife in the pack could help death along. In the next world, she'd be forgiven for that.

Dignity and pride demanded more of her, though, than just sitting around waiting to die. She recalled the expression Irish Sean Donovan used when talking about a temporary protection visa. *Ya can't just give up, Soraya. Ya gotta keep havin' a go at gettin' one.* When she asked what "havin' a go" meant, he told her. Right then, that's what she'd do. Mike the lawyer had mentioned a place called south-east Queensland, where her uncle might be. If she was going to get caught, or die, then it would happen while she was havin' a go getting there. That road to Roxby Downs was in the same direction the helicopter went. If Roxby Downs wasn't in south-east Queensland, maybe that road continued to there, or connected to another road that did. As the sun grew hotter and more flies buzzed her, she collected her things and started walking.

*

She leapt up in alarm. Belly bloated, mouth menacingly opened, it clung to the side of the rock like a magnet absorbing the day's last bit of sunlight.

She'd never seen such a huge lizard, and her first reaction was to get away fast and get down to that black ribbon of road cutting through the landscape. It was close, maybe half an hour away. But when the lizard did nothing more than flick its tongue at her, she decided to risk staying. She was exhausted, and these two rocks were the only ones in sight. So she edged back slowly and sat down, keeping a wary eye on her neighbour.

"That's your rock," she informed it in Farsi. "And this one's mine."

Frozen-eyed, only the lizard's tongue moved in response.

She got out her half-empty water bottle and took a swig. Confident now that her rock was safe, she watched twilight creep over the desert. Minutes later, a dingo howled mournfully behind her. She jerked round and scanned the ridgeline she'd just passed over. Etched against the fading light, the dingo moved along the crest, its nose down, its brush-like tail high in the air. As Soraya eased herself off the rock, the dingo stopped and stared in her direction. She reached into her pack and felt for the knife, not taking her eyes off the animal. The dingo turned and trotted back up where it came from, pausing long enough to look back before vanishing.

Relieved, she got out a slice of bread and munched it slowly, watching night come on and feeling the chill set in. She replaced her hat with a scarf and, facing the last splinter of red light on the horizon, knelt down and prayed as all other desert Moslems would do at this time of day.

Afterwards, she got into her sleeping bag and slid deep down. "The end of day two and I'm still free," she muttered, her mind flashing back to the riot. But being out here was nothing to start chanting about. She knew that, if she didn't find water in the next couple of days, her brief encounter with freedom would end in death; her body left to feed the animals out here, her bones to bleach in the sun.

Seventeen

"Day four," Soraya mumbled, trying to divert her mind. Or was it day five? As she backed away, she tried to rein in her panic by concentrating on the previous night and what she'd said to herself then. It didn't work. Her mind just wouldn't budge from the image of that thick snake slithering into a clump of pale scrub. Without breaking her gaze, she lifted the water bottle to her sun-split lips and swallowed hot air, remembering then that there hadn't been any water in the bottle since…well, since today, anyway.

She stopped. There were two choices, and going straight wasn't one of them. To her right lay another bone white salt plain, to her left more red earth and a jelly-like mirage current that screened the road. She'd heard the sound of vehicles from that directon, so she knew the road was over there somewhere. When she'd first heard those sounds, she dropped down on her hands and knees, fearing discovery. But that got difficult as the pain of her blistered feet, her thirst, spells of dizziness and bone-numbing exhaustion worsened. The past few hours, her suffering exceeded her fear of being seen. Hearing a vehicle over there now, she simply stood still until the noise disappeared. Twice this morning she'd dropped her pack on the ground and walked away before returning to retrieve it. Whatever day it was, she knew there was unlikely to be another one unless she found water soon. There was no chance of doing that on the salt plain. So, checking that the snake hadn't left the scrub, she turned left and started pushing that mirage towards the road.

*

She heard it getting louder. If she was going to avoid it, she had about five seconds to get off the side of the road. Who was she fooling? Scurrying away would just take too much energy – energy she couldn't afford to lose. So she kept going straight, her eyes fixed on the waves of heat rising off the bitumen.

With smoke funnelling out of its back end, a big car roared past in a blast of hot air and exhaust that nearly blew Soraya's hat off. Holding it on, she watched the car suddenly lurch and veer off to the side of the road, where it shuddered, spat gravel and screeched to a stop. The back door swung open. She gathered up her courage and moved towards it, her mind struggling to collect the words and phrases for questions she was sure to be asked. Drawing level, she noticed the circles of rust, and wire – like stitching – that held parts of the car together.

"Hop in, mate."

She dropped the pack on the back seat and slid in next to it, her feet landing on a carpet of crunched cans littering the floorboard. Before she'd closed the door, the car roared off.

"Where ya headed?" the big, red-faced man in the passenger seat asked, twisting around.

"Above my body" was the first answer that came to her. That couldn't be right, though. Like "flat", "headed" had a second meaning; she'd heard it. Either "going to" or "coming from". She tried the first one. "I am going to see my friend in Roxby Downs."

As he straightened up and squinted at her, she read the words scrawled across his stained T-shirt – MY WIFE HAS A DRINKING PROBLEM. ME.

"I'll be stuffed, Mitch! Under that hat sits a sheila."

"Jillaroo," was Mitch's first word, as he glanced up at her in the rear-view mirror, like Sam had days earlier. "Lookin' like 'er horse 'as given 'er the toss."

"Or camel, maybe, judgin' by how much of the Simpson she's got stuck to 'er." He finished off his beer, crunched up the can and dropped it on others. "Roxby Downs, eh?" he went on, reaching into a container in front of him. "Well, you're almost there. Just a coupla six-packs away." He took out two more cans, popped them open and handed one to Mitch and one to her. "You're lookin' drier than a dead dingo's donger back there. Here, this'll fix ya up."

"Thank you."

He nodded, keeping his eyes on her. "Ya gotta name?"

"Sarah."

"Well, Sarah, this here's Mitch and I'm Sir Francis Frederick Fullasaboot."

"I am pleased to meet you."

"Yeah. Likewise." His eyes stayed on her a bit longer, before he exchanged a quizzical look with Mitch. He got another can out for himself and seconds later looked around again. "Fred. Call me Fred."

"Yes, Fred."

The car stayed smack in the middle of the road, only veering off when an oncoming car approached. They were going even faster than she had in Sam's car. Beads of cold water fell from the can onto her hand, diverting her thoughts. She licked the beads dry, then started gulping the contents of the can. Liquid turned to froth and burned going down her throat. Grimacing, she jerked her head towards the open window, certain that what she drank was about to come back up. A sticky, bitter taste formed in her mouth as liquid hung somewhere between her throat and stomach. It was like nothing she'd ever drunk before – and tasted terrible. Even more troubling was the thought that it might contain alcohol, which was forbidden to her. "Maybe there is water?" she asked, after the liquid finally settled and she faced the front again.

"Water?" Fred exclaimed, as if she'd asked for rat poison. He took another long gulp from his can and looked back at her. "Drink too much of that and you'll rust. Don'tcha like your grog?" He looked insulted.

"Yes. It's very good. But…"

"All right, tell ya what I'll do. There's a bit of old water floatin' around in the esky down 'ere. Finish off what ya got, pass up your tinny and I'll get ya some. Got nothin' else around 'ere to put water in."

They finished off their cans, crunched them up and tossed them down. Fred opened two more, passing one to Mitch.

Soraya looked down at the can pressed between her legs, then glanced up at the back of Fred's head and the rear-view mirror. Heart thumping away, she lifted the can to the open window and tipped the grog out very carefully.

Moments later, Mitch's eyes were in that mirror again. "Not your usual sort of transport pick-up spot where ya was, back there on the road. You lost?"

She'd rehearsed for this. "A person give me a ride at Woomera. But his car makes strange noises. He stops and says he has to go back to Woomera to fix his car. Because I am late to see my friend, I say I will get out and walk, maybe another car give me a ride."

"Bugger me stiff. Sounds like heads need fixin' up before any cars do. Ya can fry your brain on the Simpson. How long ya been out there?"

"Last night and today," she lied.

Mitch belched. "And ya survived. Must have some boong in ya," he said.

She had no idea what he was talking about.

"Or Afghan?" Fred followed up.

Alarmed, Soraya looked out at the scattered anthills, pretending she didn't hear. She'd cooled off. Now, if she could just get some of that water to drink, then get them to stop, weak though she felt, those hanging bellies of theirs still made her think they wouldn't be fast enough to catch her.

Fortunately, Fred didn't seem interested in pursuing her Afghan background. "From the looks of ya, anyway," he went on, "a bit more time out there and ya could've passed yourself off as one of them anthills."

Fred and Mitch laughed together before making short work of their cans and pitching them on the floor.

Soraya leaned forward and handed her empty can to Fred. "Please. There is water?"

"Got the taste for it now, have ya, missus? Sure you won't go another tinny? Do ya the world of good, ya know."

"Maybe later," she said. Her eyes were riveted on that esky as they had been on the snake earlier.

Fred shook his head despairingly and took the can. "Ya come from anywhere round 'ere?" he asked, plunging the can in the esky and letting it fill up.

"Adelaide."

The two of them exchanged glances again.

"We're just comin' back from there," Mitch noted, his voice slurring slightly. "Put three nights in at the Breakknock Hotel. Ya know it?"

"No."

"Ah… Been livin' in Adelaide long, then?"

"One year."

Fred passed the can back to her before reaching in for more tinnies. No sooner had he popped them than Soraya was holding out her can again and asking politely for more water.

"Ya could fill the hump of a camel with that thirst of yours," he noted, lowering her can back into the esky. Giving her the can back half-filled, he winked and added, "Not much left. Get that one down ya and you'll qualify for another grog cure while the rest of the ice melts. Shouldn't take long."

She drank the water as fast as they drank their grog.

Anthills had disappeared. There was just the bright blue sky and flat red earth out there now.

"Apparently there was a bit of a kafuffle back there at the Woomera Detention Centre a few days ago," Fred mentioned after a while, not looking round. "A feral army lobbed up there, so the story goes, screamin' and carryin' on like a mob a mad galahs. They ended up bangin' a few bars limp – limp enough, anyway, for some towel-heads to slip through and disappear into the Simpson like smoke on a windy day. Hear anything about that in Adelaide, Sarah?"

Getting the gist of what he was saying, her throat nearly pinched shut. "No." She'd say she had to go to the toilet. That was it. They'd have no choice but to stop. And then she'd be able to get well away, out of sight, before they realised she wasn't coming back. Though they could get suspicious if she took her bag with her, couldn't they?

"Ya reckon any of them towel-heads are out there now chasin' up the camels?" Mitch asked Fred, as he scanned the landscape, bleary-eyed.

"Yeah, I reckon. And, with any luck at all, fallin' over and breakin' their necks as well."

They swigged away.

"So Sarah, where was ya before ya went to Adelaide?"

"Sydney."

"Oh right, and before that? I mean, your brogue's still a week or two short of bein' true blue, wouldn't ya say?"

She had no idea how to answer that.

Mitch slowed the car down. "You'll have ta press the pause button a sec, mate. M'flood gate's on overflow."

"What! Roxby's only a coupla' tinnies away."

"Won't get there. I'm bustin'. Gotta drain the screamin' dragon here and now."

"Plannin' ta drink with the flies out there, are ya?" Fred asked Mitch as the car came to a stop.

"It'd only go stale in 'ere."

"Then I'll keep ya company."

"Bewdy."

Tinnies in hand, they got out and stood together by the side of the road, swigging and urinating.

"Ooohhh. This is gooood!"

"I have to go to the toilet too," Soraya called out, shocked that they were doing such a thing in full view. She jumped into the front seat, grabbed the bottle out of her bag and dipped it quickly into the esky. She managed to get it half full again before getting out the driver's door.

"Ooohhh, yes, yes, yes! Hope it's as good for you, Sarah, as it is for us," Fred called back to her, having no idea where she'd gone.

*

Kneeling in prayer hours later, Soraya heard a dingo howl in the distance. After she finished, she muttered, "Day four and I'm still free, Mama." She got the last slice of bread out of her bag, picked the mould off it and ate watching dusk settle over the desert.

Eighteen

Soraya sat on a tree-shaded bench outside the shop. So absorbed was she in devouring her fresh bread and guzzling her bottle of cold water, she paid scant attention to the big woman – wearing a straw hat and a yellow dress – who came out of the shop with bags of food and plopped down beside her. Still thirsty, Soraya went back in, bought another bottle of water and returned to see the woman still there, her fleshy pink face beaming over at her.

"Saved your spot."

There was no one else around to save it from. Soraya thanked her anyway.

"Been down in the mines, have ya?" the woman continued.

The man in the shop had asked the same question. Averting her eyes and shaking her head seemed the right response with him, so she did the same thing again.

The woman took out a drink, punctured the top with a straw and sucked on it for a while. "From around here, are ya?

She was getting used to these abbreviated questions. "No." She took the top off the new bottle of water and drank a mouthful, making a point of scanning the road and what there was beyond it. Roxby Downs was bigger than Woomera, but had the same oasis-like streets, glinting metal-roofed houses, trees, green grass and colourful flowers. Tired though she was, those flowers still intrigued her. Before leaving Afghanistan, she'd only seen such bright colours in clothing, never in plant life. Somewhere nearby had to be wells with water to feed that colour.

"So where ya headed?"

Walking the last fifteen minutes on the road into Roxby Downs, she'd seen a sign that said, Roxby Downs 1, Marree 352. She'd practised saying the name of that other place and now felt relieved she had. "I am headed to Marree to see a friend."

"Walkin' or ridin'?"

The woman had to know how far Marree was. Soraya wondered if this was turning into more than just an exchange of words between two strangers sharing the same bench. "Some people give me a ride in their cars," she said, putting the top back on her bottle.

"Ah, good. Safer that way. Up from Woomera, are ya?"

Soraya stowed her food and drink and lifted the pack up to the bench. "Adelaide." She wanted to take off her shoes and socks, stretch her blistered feet out into the sunlight and maybe even curl up and sleep, but not with this woman next to her. Hopefully, there'd be another shady spot somewhere close by, maybe even a pool of water to bathe her feet in.

She stood up to go. "Goodbye."

"I'm headed to Marree too," the woman said, flashing a gap-toothed smile. "I'd be happy to give ya a ride there."

Thoughts of shady places and cool well water disappeared. What did Fred say? *Like smoke on a windy day.*

*

Where the township ended and the barren desert took over again, the road got rougher.

"I'm Annie," the woman said, not taking her eyes off the road.

"I am Sarah."

They bounced along in the faded, dust-covered vehicle that was somewhere between a truck and a car, like a bigger version of the one Sam drove from the cemetery to the camp site. It was square-shaped, except for the engine space, and had a grid of black iron bars jutting out at the front. The tyres were huge. They kept the vehicle high off the ground so that you had to climb up to get in. The engine growled like an angry dog and never varied. After a while, that sound started to soothe her.

"So, Sarah, this friend of yours in Marree, what's her name?

Soraya was ready for such questions. "His name is Irish Sean Donovan."

"Mmm. Can't say I've heard of him. How long's he been living in Marree?"

"One year" was what she'd rehearsed. "Only a short time," she said.

"Oh. It's a small place. For almost twenty-five years I've…" Annie stopped and glanced over at her. "Still, I'm sure there are those who do slip in and out of the place without me knowing about them. Anyway, I can drop you off at his place when we get into town."

"No worries. He says to me to use the telephone in town. He wants to come and get me."

Annie nodded her understanding. "Right… There's some tucker under your feet – sandwiches, apples, that sort of thing. Help yourself to it."

"Tucker" had to mean food. "Thank you. An apple would be very good."

"Well, grab a couple outta the bag, then, and pass one over."

Tucker certainly beat tinnies of grog, Soraya thought, as they munched on their apples and looked out at the emptiness again. Occasionally, Annie asked questions that were easy to answer. And for the first time since escaping, Soraya started to relax and feel a budding confidence that she might get to her destination after all. "South-east Queensland," she said, "can you get there from here?"

"If you're not in a hurry."

"So it is far away, then?"

"Depends whether you're travelling by car or jet aircraft."

She wouldn't be getting there today, then. Well, at least she was heading in the right direction with a good person who was offering her food and not grog.

Anthills showed again. Soraya counted thirty-two of them before a full stomach, the droning engine and hot air began to take their toll. Her eyes grew heavy. Her head started to loll.

"There's a pillow on the back seat. Why don't ya climb over, curl up and have a sleep. I'll wake ya when we get there."

Moments later, Soraya did that, and it wasn't long before she was dreaming of her Australian family in south-east Queensland.

Someone poked her then shook her. Her eyes opened. The air felt strangely cool. An engine droned away, but there was no movement. When Annie's face stretched over the front seat, her mind caught up.

"Time to wake up." Hatless, her eyes hardened, Annie looked a surprisingly different person.

"Thank you." Soraya sat up, glancing around.

Clean, sun-spattered cars were parked in lines on either side of them. Through the front windscreen, for as far as she could see, were glittering silver bars topped in razor wire: Woomera's. Horrified, she grabbed the door handle and tried to push her way out.

"Don't bother. Back doors don't work. Two ways to Marree, Sarah – or whatever your real name is. The short, rough way, or the long, smooth way down through Woomera, Port Augusta and back up again. I've got two more facts for ya, young lady. One – no one goes to south-east Queensland through Roxby Downs and Marree unless they've got a screw loose or haven't been in the country long enough to learn to read a map. Two – I work at the Marree Hotel. I know everyone in town, whether they've been there for hours or decades. And there's no one by the name of Irish Sean Donovan who's ever set foot in the place. Not a name a person would tend to forget, is it? Now, if you can show me some sort of identification, something with the name Sarah whatever and an Adelaide address on it, then we'll continue on to Marree. If not, then I'll assume you're Sore-ya somebody, an illegal boat-hugger and escapee whose name has been front-paged in all the newspapers these past few days. So, over to you. Which one are ya?"

She sat there stunned, trying to work out what to do, before climbing back in the front seat and retrieving her pack. "Soraya."

The windows were all shut. Cool air circulated from a vent near her feet.

Annie pointed. "Then get back in there where ya belong. Try running away," she warned, "and I'll be at that front gate raising the alarm before your backside's cleared the car park."

Soraya picked up the hat, wound down the window and tossed it out, then put her scarf on, tying it under her chin. "For five days I am alone in the desert, free. My best five days in Australia." Pack in hand, she opened the door, then hesitated. "When I think of Australia and people like Annie from Marree, I always think of empty hearts. Empty as the land you live in."

"Piss off."

Whatever that meant, Soraya knew it couldn't be nice. There were advantages in not speaking the same language, she thought, as she stepped down with the picture of her mother filling her mind. It brought a wistful smile to her face, before she dropped the pack, turned in the direction of the desert and started to run.

A car horn blasted, a door slammed.

"Escapee! Escapee!" Annie screamed behind her.

Soraya felt the pain of her blistered feet, but she didn't let it slow her down as she sprinted past the cars. First, her backside would clear the car park. After that, nothing else mattered.

Out on the road, she smiled and shouted, "My backside's cleared the car park, Annie!" Then laughter spilled out, high and youthful again. It felt good, but surprised her also, as though it had come from someone else close by.

Seconds later, her panting breath took over as she ran parallel with the fence line. Prisoners turned and pointed. Someone yelled out, "RUN! RUN! RUN!" like during the last riot. A chant broke out that faded the closer she got to the crossroad. To the right was the main gate, to the left more fence line. She went straight, out into the desert – her breath hot and ragged, her feet shooting pain, her legs starting to tremble. But what did it matter?

Far behind her, a man shouted, "Stop! There's nowhere to go out there!"

She barely had the breath to shout back, "There's nowhere to go back there…either." It was the first time she'd ever used that last word and the thought of her English improving, in this last, useless dash for freedom, made her smile.

Exhaustion soon slowed her to a jog then from a jog to long, determined strides. Her strides shortened and her mind zipped off somewhere else.

You and your cousin Khalida, both fourteen and still so willful.

Fut – fut – fut – fut – fut – fut… Distant at first, but closing in. Fut – fut – fut – fut…

Gunfire raked the ground. Whoosh. Whoosh. Rockets streaked to the valley floor.

Muhammed's voice was in her ear. *It's far away, Soraya – not here, not here.*

"It is, Muhammed! It is!"

Fut – fut – fut – fut… Air vibrated. A downdraft hit sending her scarf flying. Grit and sand stung her face. FUT – FUT – FUT – FUT…

She refused to look round, counting her steps instead, as she had anthills earlier, before she was hit and slammed to the ground.

"Stay right here!" a man shouted in her ear.

Her body went limp. She hurt and started to cry quietly, wanting those thrashing blades to topple over on her and put an end to everything.

Nineteen

Waiting for Mike the lawyer, Soraya looked around the interview room thinking again how well the burqa suited her feelings. It slowed her movements, kept her hidden away and narrowed her view of things. Everything seemed more distant from inside it. Though, of course, it made little difference what she wore on the bench, where Ehsan doted over her and insisted on bringing her things. She recalled her first afternoon back there, answering his questions, before the chance came to ask a couple of her own.

"I look everywhere and I cannot find Elham and Salar. Where are they?" she'd asked.

"Gone."

She discovered then that she still carried emotions. "Gone where?"

"To another prison somewhere south."

The Welcome to Woomera man approached minutes later, shaking his head. "Well, well, well, Soraya of the Simpson Desert, I presume. A bit sore and sorry, I hear, but hopefully a bit wiser also about the dangers of solo travel out there – not excluding trying to outrun helicopters." He didn't stay.

The burqa she wore once belonged to the young Iranian woman from their compound. She was somewhere south now as well. Rather than allow it to be thrown out, Soraya tried it on and decided to keep it.

Another reason for wearing the burqa soon became apparent. When the Welcome to Woomera man next appeared, she responded to his comments by continuing to gaze out at the desert and reciting the words Ehsan had given her. "When you wear a burqa, Ehsan, you're in such a private world. You see so little, or hear so little of your own voice and only what you choose to hear from others." Perhaps she was martyring herself, but wearing the burqa did put a stop to the lessons to be learned from escaping and wandering the desert.

There were certainly no problems hearing Mike the lawyer, though, as his footsteps bounded up the steps now, snapping her out of her reverie. "G'day," he greeted her in his usual energetic manner. His leather bag slapped the table and he sat down opposite her.

This was his second visit in a week. Four days earlier, they'd talked about her escape, like she'd talked about it with Ehsan. As to the chances of her ever getting a temporary protection visa, Mike the lawyer only mentioned that her chances hadn't improved. Folding his hands and resting his elbows on the table, he asked his usual questions before saying, "I've received important information from both the Afghani Embassy and the Australian government's Department of Immigration. Some of it's good news, some of it isn't." Like his habit of explaining difficult words, he always warned her when he was going to explain something important to her. "Are you ready to listen?"

"Yes."

"The good news is that your relatives from Masar e-Sharif have been located, which is more than I can say for your disappearing uncle somewhere in Australia. Anyway, they're well and living in Kabul now." He eyed her for a reaction, then realised how difficult that would be to detect. He breathed a heavy sigh. "Now, the other news… You know the Taliban no longer rule in Afghanistan and that there's a new government, being helped by the United Nations, that's trying to rebuild your country. We've talked about the United Nations, haven't we?"

So much of what she knew about the outside world, she'd learned from Muhammed, Elham and Salar and Mike the lawyer. "Yes."

"Even though there is still some fighting going on outside Kabul, the Australian government now considers Kabul a safe place for Afghan asylum seekers to return to. And that is the official reason, anyway, why our latest temporary protection visa application has been rejected. And sadly, if we don't appeal…uh, fight the decision in the next couple of days, then your name will be added to the list of asylum seekers who will soon be deported. You know what that word means, don't you?"

"Yes."

"Right… Well, then… We can appeal if you want to, Soraya. But, to be brutally honest, I think it would be a waste of time. There hasn't been a single such appeal, that I know of anyway, that's been upheld…uh, agreed to." He sat there quietly and let that sink in before asking, "How do you feel about going back to Afghanistan?"

There was no sense answering the question, because Mike the lawyer wouldn't begin to understand how much she'd failed her family; that being imprisoned here made her ashamed to be sent home, and that living with such shame could be worse than dying. "When?"

"Three, maybe four weeks."

She thought of Ehsan then, sitting on the bench, staring out at the desert, alone.

Twenty

Then get back in there where ya belong.

Soraya cast Annie's angry face out of her mind and concentrated on what was around her: clattering hoofs, creaking wheels, noisy motorbikes spilling out exhaust and the many old men and women and children sitting under tarpaulins amongst the dust and rubble. Few young Afghani men seemed to populate Kabul now. Though young, heavily armed Westerners were here, mostly crowded in the back of UN utility trucks that regularly passed by. And a thought struck her then that, like the Westerners, she was an outsider here too.

The cart driver reined in his horse and pointed to a side road crumpled up like old cake. "That's Babur Road. I can't go any further. It's too rough. The place you're looking for is about three hundred metres down the road, on the left."

Soraya knew that. Officials had told her, as they had told her everything else she needed to know. Being deported from prison was very different from being put into one. When they knew what was happening to her, every Australian she came across – except one – treated her like Irish Sean Donovan and Mike the lawyer had. They were friendly and helpful and provided heaps of information. And they were there at the prison gate and airport waving and smiling and shouting goodbye to her when she left. So in a way Pervez Lateef was right. It was just that Australians did the things he said they would do when refugees left the country, not when they arrived.

Grabbing her backpack and bag, she paid the driver and stepped down. The anxiety she'd felt flying back to Islamabad, then taking a UN truck to Kabul, didn't ease as she set off down the road now – no, not at all. As she passed older men and young boys chatting and working on bicycles, and starkly open-faced women and girls minding children and doing housework, her anxiety surged. And she began to realise that there was more to her fears than just the big task of confronting her relatives. Things had changed. Uncomfortably, so had she. Though there had certainly been bursts of night screams and violence at Woomera, stillness and monotony were the norm. As she stepped aside to let a revving motorbike pass, she thought how sensitive she'd become to the bustle and noise of city life. Certainly the open-faced women here were a comfort to her, but she knew that, even after reconciling things with her auntie and uncle, it was still going to take time to catch up with all this and to feel she really did belong in Kabul.

Muhammed entered her mind. *This storm too will pass, but within this room there will always be peace. Allah akbar.*

Soraya turned and gazed northwards into the midday haze. Vague mounds and curves on the horizon were all that showed of Muhammed's mountains. She knew they'd be clearer and look closer in the morning, and that thought kept her mind fixed on him as she moved slowly down the road.

A tea stall appeared on her left. Emerging from a huddle of stooped men there, a little girl carried a small cup of tea very carefully across the road to where a grey-bearded man squatted, filing away at a metal frame. He stopped long enough to accept the cup, wrap his arm around the little girl and say something that made her giggle, as though she'd just been tickled.

Soraya stopped and watched them.

While the man went on with his work, the little girl played with a rag doll next to him. A minute later, the man stopped to blow into his tea. When it had obviously cooled enough, he encouraged the little girl to share it with him. While he held the cup, she took a sip – seemingly for the first time – and screwed up her face, not liking it. The man laughed and drew her to him.

Soraya turned away, smiling, and looked up the road at the vague mountains again. Annie and Muhammed, eh? One with a huge car and bags of food and drink, the other with a walking stick, a little tea, rice, yoghurt and naan bread.

It struck her that up there with him was the only place in the world where she had belonged after she left Mazar-e Sharif. And she imagined climbing the mountain track and knocking on his door, and the door opening and his face beaming out. What she imagined saying to him then made her shake her head at the memory of Australia.

She looked around at the men at the tea stall and that man and little girl, before her mind started to wander again. Mustafa carried Taliban supplies to Kabul from up there. He'd know the track. He might be able to lead her up there, sometime, after she'd faced up to everyone down the road. Her mood darkened as she pictured herself trying to explain.

Going from Indonesia to Australia, we were on a small, overcrowded boat in a storm, and after the storm finally ended, a big Australian ship came alongside. Australians came on board and said everything would be fine for us in Australia and their big ship pulled us to a place called Darwin. But the Australians lied, because things weren't fine, they were really bad. We were put on a plane and sent to a prison in the middle of a desert. Many depressed and angry prisoners from Afghanistan and other countries were there. It was terrible. One day…

She stopped. Why punish herself more than she had to? She'd have to tell the entire story to her aunt and uncle soon enough but, after that, never again. Best to get there and get it over with, she thought, walking on.

Minutes later, she spotted what she was looking for — the raised section of wall and blue metal gate that separated a tiny courtyard and her relatives' one-room house from the road. Heart pounding, she went through the gate and stepped up to the door, noticing it was padlocked. She knocked anyway, then went over to the tiny window and peeked in.

Worn carpet covered most of the earthen floor. Sleeping mats, cushions and blankets were scattered about. It was going to be crowded living in there. But no more crowded than at Woomera. She sat down out of the sun, back propped against the wall, and waited for someone to arrive.

When the sun moved overhead, what shade there was soon disappeared. It got hot and she started to get thirsty, so she took out some coins and walked back up to the tea stall. She'd never bought tea amongst men without her burqa on, but the recollection of that little girl doing it boosted her confidence. Head lowered in submission, she wound her way up to the plank counter and ordered.

Moments later, a glass of tea in her hand, she retreated to where she'd stopped earlier in the day. Sampling her tea, she looked northwards again. His mountains seemed to have retreated in the time she'd spent waiting down the road.

Two planes suddenly streaked overhead. She was the only one startled enough to look up at them. No one else seemed remotely interested.

An old man with a walking stick came away from the stall and stood slurping his tea next to her. He reminded her of Muhammed, and perhaps because of that, a question slipped from her mouth.

"Those mountains," she asked timidly, using her head as a pointer, "are they very far away?"

The old man looked from the mountains to her and shook his head slowly. "Pay the cart man a little extra and he'd get you up to the start of the track in under an hour. Do you know someone in those mountains?"

"I have a friend – a rohani – who lives up there."

His eyes brightened. A grin deepened his wrinkles. "Would the friend be named Muhammed?"

The delight in her smile carried to her eyes. "Yes! You know him! How is he? Have you seen him lately? Is he still living in his hut up there?"

"To answer your questions in the order they were asked: yes, years ago we lived in the same village. Reports I've heard say he's fine. No. Yes, he apparently is." He slurped his tea, dribbling a bit on his beard, before looking over at her again. "Now, that done, I've got a question for you. Some time ago, I heard he was with a young person, about your age, walking the mountain track towards Pakistan. You don't know who that young person may have been, do you?"

She knew he knew she did. "Me."

"By name?"

"Soraya Zadran."

"Ah then, Soraya Zadran, tell me how long it's been since you made that journey with him." It must have been obvious to him why she'd made the journey.

"About a year ago…I think."

"That's a long time for an old man to be away from good friends, even if he is a rohani." He finished his tea. "It sounds to me like you should get up there and visit him. Insha'allah."

Her eyes dropped. "Balay. Sometime."

"Sometime could be a long time, perhaps too long a time."

Was there a message in that? "You did say he was fine, didn't you?"

"Mmm, I did… For now, anyway." He turned and went back to the stall. Minutes later, he returned with another full cup. "So, are you living around here now, Soraya Zadran?"

She told him where her relatives were living and that she'd come to Kabul to stay with them. She didn't explain why.

"Ah, then you've missed them. I know your uncle. He was at this stall yesterday morning. He said he and his family were going to Kowl-o Ashrow. It's an hour's bus ride to the west. Just where they are there, I don't know. But it's a small place. So if you went there and asked around, I'm sure you'd find them. Of course, in the same time it would take for you to do that, you could be well up the mountain track. Insha'allah."

That picture of her at his door formed again. "Are there still landmines in those mountains? Is the fighting still going on?"

"The landmines on the track, anyway, have been cleared. And I've not heard of any fighting up there since the Taliban supposedly left. Of course, Afghanis being who they are, and the fact that there are so many foreign soldiers in the area carrying guns in the name of peace, there's nowhere that's entirely safe, not even Kabul."

What a coincidence, meeting this old man who knew Muhammed so well. But then, with her relatives away, there was another way of viewing their meeting – as a clear sign that she was destined to return to Muhammed's mountains. Her feet had healed. And, after all the walking she'd done in the desert, she was confident the climb wouldn't be difficult for her. Besides, she had a good pack and enough money to buy some food before she started. So she could go as slowly as she wanted to.

"Iqbal, my nephew, lives very close to the start of the track. He has rooms he rents. His place is called Iqbal's Inn. You could stay there the night and start the climb early in the morning. Good idea, I think. Just give Iqbal my name – Uncle Tariq. And if you tell him you're going to visit Muhammed, he'll draw you a map and you'll pay very little money for your room, if anything."

So strong was his encouragement that Soraya wondered if he was hiding something from her. But if Muhammed were sick, that was even greater reason to visit him, wasn't it? And since no one was here for her at the moment, now was the best time to do it. The idea gripped her, displacing everything else in her mind. "I'm very happy I've talked to you," she said to Uncle Tariq. "I will stay at your nephew's and tomorrow I will go up and visit Muhammed. Insha'allah."

*

Counting steps had become a habit in prison and quickly became one here too. Climbing up the steep track, Soraya vowed she'd only stop to rest after completing one hundred and eighteen big steps, the number from Woomera's main compound to their bench. Then, if she chose not to stop, she had to do the same number of steps before she was allowed the choice again. And part of the joy she felt in doing this came from the fact that she was free and, unlike at Woomera, each lot of one hundred and eighteen steps took her higher and closer to the one place where she knew she belonged.

Joy also came from recalling Muhammed's voice in her ear, confirming that these mountains held no fear for her any more. Her body and mind were working as one, as he said they should. Though her breathing was audible, her legs felt strong. She was pacing herself well. She drank a little water, ate a little food and filled her mind with what there was to see – the things he'd pointed out to her before.

The gorge, so narrow the rocks nearly touch overhead. The mountains towering up, cradling the valley in their hands. *This is about as close as we'll ever get, Soraya, to God's view of the world. There on that boulder is the letter M. M for Muhammed, M for Mustafa, so you will always know where to find shelter.*

And she suspected he knew she'd be returning and that now there would be an S on that boulder as well. She was getting close. It wouldn't be long before she found out.

The padding of running feet and the sound of panting breath beat the air suddenly. She wheeled around just as a man carrying a rifle – his black robe trailing in the breeze – dashed past her, going in the same direction. Others quickly followed. Alarmed, she stopped and looked down the valley where lines of fighters were scurrying up tracks towards the ridge. They were Taliban, all of them, and so intent were they on getting to where they were going, they completely ignored her. And moments later she learned why.

Fut – fut – fut – fut – fut – fut… Up the valley they came, her nightmare returning.

God's close world suddenly shrunk to M for Muhammed. As groups of fighters sprinted past her, she dropped her things and ran with them, searching frantically for that boulder and the corridor to Muhammed's hut.

Fut – fut – fut – fut – fut – fut… Helicopters cut across the sky. One banked in over them.

Tat – tat – tat – tat – tat – tat…

All she could do was run, run fast, faster than she'd run at Woomera, faster than she ever thought she could run, searching, searching, searching and crying out, "No closer! Please! No closer!"

FUT – FUT – FUT – FUT – FUT – FUT…

She dived down.

TAT – TAT – TAT – TAT – TAT – TAT… Bullets slapped and ricocheted around her.

When the helicopter veered back over the valley, she sprang up, leapt over a blood-smeared fighter and raced on.

Rounding a bend with the sound of another helicopter closing in fast, her eyes lit up. She saw it as the biggest single letter she'd ever seen, on the face of the most beautiful boulder in the world, maybe twenty metres away. Then she saw another M, then an S on the same boulder and, crazily, the laugh that had spilled out in the car park weeks earlier did so again as she heard Annie's voice ringing out above the rotor blades and bullets. *Then get back in there where ya belong.*

"I am! I am!"

FUT – FUT – FUT – FUT- FUT – FUT…

Her laughter froze.

TAT – TAT – TAT – TAT – TAT…

Cracked in shade and widening out, the corridor was only seconds away.

TAT – TAT – TAT – TAT – TAT – TAT…

Ducking down, she zipped past the boulder and cut into the corridor with just enough breath to scream out, "MUHAMMED!"

WHOOSH!

*

First the cold, as if her bones lay on ice. Then the ringing in her ears – throbbing and spreading as pain to her head, chest and legs. Her eyes opened to shimmering light. No movement, no sounds – just that light and the cold and the pain. She wanted to know more. She wanted to turn her head and see where she was – Afghanistan, Woomera, paradise, hell. But her body refused to cooperate – going heavy, shutting her eyes, dropping her back into the void that carried her away.

Next time – dull light, grey boulders above two faces looking down at her. One belonged to Muhammed. The other one was black-bearded and turbaned and had severe, deep-set eyes. Taliban. Hell. So why was Muhammed next to him? He wasn't really there, was he? Hell was intent on tormenting her. She closed her eyes and prayed for the void.

Again – ringing ears and pain, yes, but dulled in the warmth and confined lamplight. And more – a cushion under her head, a blanket spread over her, wood smoke and a cracking fire. Her body wanted this, her head turned. Muhammed – only Muhammed – sat cross-legged next to her reading his Koran. Afghanistan, or paradise? It didn't matter. Both were the same inside the sanctuary of his hut. Her mind opened further. Memory flowed.

"Towards God is the journeying, Muhammed," she said quietly, "the journeying back."